CHAMELEON

AND OTHER STORIES

JANE BRYCE

CHAMELEON

AND OTHER STORIES

PEEPAL TREE

First published in Great Britain in 2007
Peepal Tree Press Ltd
17 King's Avenue
Leeds LS6 1QS
England

ISBN 1 84523 041 8
ISBN13: 9 781 84523 041 8

Acknowledgement toFela Anikulapo-Kuti for his songs
'Lady' and 'Beasts of No Nation'.

 Peepal Tree gratefully acknowledges Arts Council support

CONTENTS

I

The Prayer Rug   7

Chameleon   17

Mariamu and the Demon   24

Marangu   33

'Almost Like England'   38

The Other Letter She Did Not Write   43

Maria Morphopolous's Slipper   49

II

The Road   61

Masquerade   67

'Lady'   73

III

Looking for Òsun:

    1.   The Town and the Sacred Grove   95

    2.   Carnival   100

    3.   Luis   110

For Mary, Ally and Sally – 'those others'

THE PRAYER RUG

Home was a long way from the Coast. Driving back after the seaside holiday was hot and boring, without the excitement of going away and the sea and all its adventures to look forward to. It was hard when her back was burnt and peeling so she couldn't sit still, but she had to try to keep from bumping the seat in front of her. This year, though, there was the rug. Rolled up on the back seat to keep it out of the dust, its faint, musty fragrance held vague promises of things to come.

Her father had been so excited when he saw the notice 'Carpet Auction', and her mother explained it was a sale, and the carpets came from Persia and India. They had gone to the place; it was in the old part of the city, with all the carved wooden doors and little windows high up with iron bars. She stayed close to her mother because it wasn't like anywhere she had been before; she wasn't sure of the smell or the narrow streets and the people in their long robes. Inside the auction it was ordinary again; Indian merchants like the ones at home showing you the carpets in a big room; then you sat down and they brought you hot sweet tea on a brass tray. The carpets smelt, not bad but different, rich, as if they had come from far away and brought the smell with them. A man stood up at the front, calling out things and people called back, and her father called too and at the end of it, they left with three rolled-up carpets which one of the Indian merchant's sons carried to the car. Two of the carpets had to go on the roof-rack, they were

7

too big for inside; only the small one shared the back seat with her. It felt like hers. The parents were happy and it made her feel grown-up, being there, hearing them talk about the auction. 'That Mori prayer rug,' said the father, 'a beautiful piece of work. You don't get a chance like that very often.' 'And the colours, that blue and that red,' said the mother. 'Like jewels.'

She knew they wouldn't go straight home to the holiday house on the beach. It was an excuse for celebration, bottles of Tusker beer and a coke for her, spicy samosas which she loved, fresh roasted groundnuts, maybe an ice-cream. But she wanted to see the rug unrolled, to look at the colours, like jewels, to feel its softness. Mori prayer rug. Her mother explained that Muslims prayed on rugs like that, kneeling towards Mecca, their holy place. The other carpets were patterned all over, the same pattern repeating, with a bright border, one red, one blue. A matching pair. But the rug was different; it had the shape of an arch at one end only. If you held it up it could be a doorway. 'The gateway to Paradise,' the mother explained. 'When you pray, you pass through the gateway.'

The child thought of Ahmed, the garden boy at home. He was a Muslim, and he was from the Coast. On Friday afternoons, he didn't come to work because he had to go to the mosque in town. She used to watch him leave in his special clothes, like the ones in the old town when they bought the carpets. Once, her mother was driving into town, and they gave him a lift. At the mosque she saw him join a crowd of men taking off their shoes on the steps. Friday afternoon was the only time she ever saw him in shoes. The rest of the time, he was barefoot and wearing tattered khaki shorts which were too big for him. She craned her neck as they drove away, but she didn't know when he went inside, or what he did there. She knew Allah was inside. More than once, she had stayed in his room while he prayed, but she had never seen him enter Paradise. Perhaps he needed a rug. Ahmed prayed on a mat facing the wall.

8

The car spun out the miles in a skein of red dust. Sunburn was easier if you propped yourself on your knees and stared out of the back window, watching the circular swirl of dust, like water going down the plughole in the bath at home. If you were lucky, there might be animals, perhaps a giraffe loping away in the distance, or gazelles peeping from the long savannah grass. Even something dangerous – an elephant, a rhino – but that was rare, and usually only at dusk, not in the early morning. So you counted the wooden telegraph poles, strung together with a dip in the middle and up at both ends, mile after mile of them, till you got to a hundred and got confused, or sleepy. After hours and hours, they would stop for breakfast at the side of the road, with tea in a thermos that didn't taste like tea, and sandwiches you never felt like eating, because car travel made you sick. Sometimes you *were* sick, and you'd better make sure you said so in time for the car to stop so you didn't do it all over the back seat. But very very slowly the sun would start to fall down the other side of the sky, and you sat up again, waiting for the first glimpse of the mountain, the first familiar landmarks at the edge of town, the turning off the main road, the drive-way. Then you were home, falling gratefully out of the car, stretching aching legs, in a frenzy of barking and patting and romping and things being taken bit by bit into the house.

And now, the rug was home. She watched it being carried inside by Antony, the houseboy. She followed him, saw where he put it, on the floor of the sitting room, watched as her father unrolled it, shook it out and laid it down in front of the fire place. Antony wouldn't know about it, he was a Christian and knelt in church just like they did, not on a rug. Mori. Allah. Paradise. Jewels. She couldn't wait to see Ahmed.

She found Ahmed in the garden, where he always was, squatting by a flower-bed, carefully planting seedlings with a trowel. He said nothing when she joined him, squatting silently beside him and watching as he dribbled water into the holes he'd made. She knew if she waited he would let her help, but she shouldn't ask. She followed him around for half the morning, carrying the watering can, heavy at first, becoming lighter and lighter as they progressed. When she saw him glance at the sky, she knew it was time to stop, and she had earned the right to follow him to his room and watch him eat.

She was allowed to taste his food too, but today she was too full of her story.

'Ahmed, we went to an auction. It was in Mombasa. We bought carpets, and a Mori prayer rug. How do you pray with it? Do you enter Paradise?' He looked at her, smiling at her excitement. 'Mombasa', he said. 'That's close to where I come from.' He had told her before about his home. It was an island, Pemba, not as big as Zanzibar, but far more beautiful. He had left it when he was very young and grown up in Tanga, on the Coast. Because there were too many children, his father had sent him to live with his uncle upcountry, and his uncle had come to her father to ask him if he needed a garden boy. The child knew Ahmed's uncle too; he worked at her father's office, and he always talked to her when she went there to spend an afternoon. Once a year, he and Ahmed went home to Tanga. It was far, she knew how far, and she was sorry that Ahmed only saw his family then. But Ahmed didn't seem to mind. He said it was the will of Allah. Allah lived at the mosque, but he could hear Ahmed's prayers even from his room at home.

'Ahmed, when you pray, do you enter Paradise? Where is it?' He was silent, and his face became mysterious, in a way that was familiar to her. He knew wonderful stories, but you couldn't make him tell them. Sometimes when she asked a question, he would just stay quiet, as if he hadn't heard. Other times, he would talk and talk, and she didn't understand half of what he said. He would talk about his family at the Coast, about Pemba and the spirits who lived there, who were very powerful. He knew things no-one else knew, even how to read the funny letters in the Koran. It was a big book like the

Bible, but the writing was different, and when he read he started at the end and read backwards. Sometimes he read to her, the sounds falling all around like music.

'Paradise,' he said. 'Paradise is a garden. It has rivers, and a fountain, and when you go there, you wear silk clothes and drink out of silver and crystal.' 'Where is it, Ahmed?' the child asked carefully. 'We cannot find it on earth,' he replied. 'But every garden reminds us of it and that we should try to be good, so we can go there one day.' 'Does our garden remind you?' she asked him. 'Yes, but it is work. Kazi sana. In Paradise, young maidens do the work and the faithful rest.' 'Will I go there too?' she asked.

He was silent, then he shook his head. 'You are a Christian,' he said. 'Christians have their own place.'

For a moment she was stricken, but then she remembered. 'Ahmed, can I show you the rug?' she asked. 'It's beautiful, its colours are like jewels.' He laughed. 'Ask the memsahib' was all he would say. She knew it was time for him to rest, and she should go, but she lingered, unsatisfied. 'Go now,' he said. 'I will meet you in Paradise.' She went.

Antony was cleaning inside, and had put the rug out on the verandah. She had waited several days, hoping this would happen. Ahmed had said to ask her mother, but she didn't like to in case she said no. Her world was full of incomprehensible prohibitions: don't cut centipedes in half, don't ride the bicycle outside the garden, don't disturb the servants when they're working. Mostly she did she what she wanted when no-one was watching. She and Ahmed were digging a watercourse from the furrow to the flower bed on the top terrace, because he had said Paradise was a garden full of rivers, and theirs had none. In the rains, the furrows which circled the garden beyond the hedge were full and rushing with water. Now, they were down to a trickle, but a thunderstorm could come any time, and they would be ready. They had dug for days. It had been her idea, but Ahmed had welcomed it. He said it would

11

save on the hose water. She ran towards him, stumbling a little on the terrace, out of breath.

'Ahmed, please come. The rug is on the verandah,' she panted. He looked up from the hard dry earth he was hacking with a panga to loosen it. He glanced towards the house. He knew its rhythm as well as she, knew the parents were both out and they had nothing to fear, but unlike her, he didn't take risks with prohibitions. He was the garden boy, and the house was not his domain. Today, however, the work they had been doing together had pleased him, and he wanted to please her in return. Together they approached the verandah, stopping just inside the patch of shade cast by the overhanging roof, in the shadow of the house but still outside its confines. They looked at the rug, spread haphazardly on the low concrete balustrade. Eagerly, she looked at his face, but could see nothing against the bright glare of the light behind him. When he spoke, his hushed voice surprised her.

'That's the mihrab,' he said reverentially, pointing to the rug. 'The archway which points the way to Mecca. It's on the wall of the mosque too, so we know which way to look when we pray. It's the gateway of the Prophet, who stands in the door of God. When we pray, all together at the same time, we join with Muslims all over the world who are all thinking of Allah. Then we are on the threshold.'

She did not understand his words. Mihrab. Threshold. But he had seen it, that was enough. He had shared it with her. Until he had seen it, it had held its secret away from her, but now she knew he would tell her more. She only had to prompt him. Shyly, she caught his hand and pulled him backwards, knowing Antony would come soon and catch them. He stepped abruptly back into the brightness, his shorts falling below his belly button. Like him, she was in shorts and barefoot. Together, they trudged back up the garden, and squatted on the parched earth under the flame tree. He picked up a fallen seed pod and scratched a line in the dirt.

'Threshold,' he said. 'The door is like this line. One step and you're across it. But to cross, you must know many things, you must be worthy to enter Paradise. If you are not wise enough yourself, you can ask for help. In Pemba, we have a mighty spirit we can call on. He is one of the djinn who helped Solomon build the arches in the temple, like the archway on the prayer rug. When Solomon died, they went all over the earth, and a very powerful one came to Pemba.'

She wanted to ask, *What are djinn?* But she didn't dare interrupt the flow of his words, like water. Instead, she stored them in her mind, where she could sip at them slowly. Threshold. Spirit. Djinn. Mihrab. The words accumulated, pregnant with power. Jewels. She heard his voice resume, still in that hushed tone that was barely above a whisper.

'We are taught that man is made of clay, like this earth.' His fingers scraped the dry ground, his fingernails red with dust. 'It was Allah who breathed the spirit into Adam, and our djinn is part of the breath of Allah. In Swahili we say, *p'epo.* It means spirit, breath, Paradise, all three. When we *punga p'epo*, we call the spirit, and it fills us up inside.' Ahmed laid his hands flat, red with dust, over his belly button. 'I have seen it. The women speak with the djinn's voice. They are able to cross the threshold. The rest of us can only watch.'

The heat, the smell of the earth, the brilliance of the light, the incantation of words whose meanings eluded her, filled the child with a kind of ecstasy, and her head swam. Ahmed brought his gaze to rest on her flushed face, and smiled. 'You must go inside now, small memsahib,' he ordered. 'These things are heavy, and they are only for you. Because of the prayer rug. They are our secret. Even in the mosque, we do not speak of them. There are people who believe that djinn are evil, that when they open their mouths towards heaven, their breath stinks so bad the angels can't bear it, and so they ask Allah to grant the prayer quickly to stop the smell. They say it's wrong to pray like that, because it molests the angels.

13

But we know that our djinn protects us, and breathes the breath of Allah into us.'

Ahmed rose, and in a reversal of the previous gesture, held out his hand to pull her to her feet. She staggered a little, the blood all in her feet, sun and shadow dancing across her vision. Then she went to the house.

She was in disgrace. What she dreaded most, her father's anger, had descended on her, and she still smarted from his hand on her bare legs. Locked in her room at one end of the house, she had wept so much her throat was swollen, and her breath came in hiccups that threatened to choke her. She had tried to explain, to no avail. Her words seemed to carry no meaning; no-one wanted to hear. 'It was the archway,' she wailed. 'You go through it to reach Paradise. You have to pray and the spirit fills you, then you can pass through. He only has a wall, I wanted him to have the archway…'

They had found the prayer rug in Ahmed's room while he was at the mosque. She had carried it there when she saw him leave, in his kanzu and sandals and, less than an hour later, Antony had come to report to her mother that it was missing. Theft was a serious thing, especially by a member of the household. Her mother had waited for her father to come home, and he had decreed a search of the servants' quarters. At first, she had stayed quiet, paralysed with fear, as they discussed what to do with Ahmed on his return.

'He'll have to go. We can't have him entering the house like that, let alone taking things. And a carpet…' 'But if it means something in his religion, can't we warn him this time? He probably didn't see it as stealing.' Her father always got impatient with her mother when she made excuses for the servants. 'Don't be silly, they all know what stealing is. You have to make an example when this kind of thing happens. You can't afford to be soft.' Her mother, who shared the house and the garden with Antony and Ahmed, clung to her own version. 'But he's never done anything like this before, and he's such a good shamba boy. I don't know where I'll find someone who's so good with plants again.'

It was a while before she realised what it meant. They thought Ahmed had stolen the rug, and they were going to send him away. She knew she had to speak, but it was a while before she could find the words. She waited till her mother was alone, and whispered it in her ear. She and Mummy had secrets from Daddy, and she begged her not to tell, but Mummy looked sad and said it was too serious and she had to tell him or Ahmed would suffer. Daddy was very angry. He was cold and hard, and he took her by the wrist and dragged her round to the back of the house. She was afraid of him, the way she had to run to keep up with him, the way he looked straight ahead and his mouth was a thin, straight line. It hurt when he hit her, but what hurt more was that he didn't want to listen. As if she wasn't there, as if there wasn't a reason for what she had done. Ahmed needed the rug; it was the archway. Daddy said she nearly got Ahmed the sack, and what on earth possessed her to be in his room? Then he locked her up, and she heard the car leaving and knew her parents had gone to the club. She listened to the silence and felt the heat in the bedroom lie on her skin, making it hard to breathe. She was still locked up when it began to rain.

She had not seen the lightning flash at first, but she heard the thunder through her wails. The first crack split the sky apart, and she screamed in terror. Antony would be in the kitchen, but she was all alone. It had never happened before. When there was a thunderstorm, she would be with her mother, and they would hold each other as they watched the lightning, and she would feel safe. But to be alone, in a locked room, and oh! She screamed again as the thunder boomed and the house shook, and then the rain came. A curtain suddenly fell between her and the garden, so heavy was the rain, beating on the rooftiles, flinging itself at the earth. She shivered and trembled, weeping at its ferocity, but her sobs were drowned in the downpour. It grew dark, but she was too weak to leave the window, immobilised by misery. To

15

comfort herself, she placed her two hands flat on her belly, as she had seen Ahmed do that day in the garden. She breathed the words she had heard him speak – djinn, mihrab, threshold – as if summoning a powerful spirit. Mesmerised by the fall of water, numbed by the sound of its drumming on the ground, she was startled back into terror by a voice speaking very close to her. It seemed to come from inside the room, and she looked around wildly, but saw nothing. It spoke again, barely a murmur, and now she knew it came from the gloom outside.

'Small memsahib, it is me. Ahmed. Don't be afraid. I heard what happened, and that they locked you up. They will be back soon, but I am here now. Don't cry any more. I am here.' Ahmed. She strained her eyes and could just make him out, pressed up against the mosquito netting of the window, sheltering as best he could between the wall of rain pouring from the overhanging roof and the rough exterior wall of the house. He must have come back from the mosque and Antony would have told him the story. Did he know she nearly got him the sack? Did he know her father beat her?

'It's all right, memsahib kidogo. I heard about the rug. It was wrong to take it, but you told the truth and you should not have been punished for it. But don't worry, Allah knows. He is everywhere and he will protect you. Did you hear the thunder? That was his voice. He has sent a blessing to the garden. The rain will fill the furrow, and water will flow along our channel, and the garden will have a river, just like we said. Tomorrow, when they go to work, we will visit our Paradise.'

Outside, Ahmed shivered, wet to the skin and frozen. Inside, the child clung to the window bars, absorbing his voice. Neither of them knew when the car returned, the crunch of tyres on the gravel obliterated by the rain. But the child heard the bolt shoot back on the outside of the door, and turned, and saw her mother, her tennis dress streaked with rain, drops of water in her hair. The tennis racquet dropped to the floor as the child flung herself, wild, upon her mother.

CHAMELEON

If not for Ahmed, she would have missed it. She was helping in the garden, or rather hanging around him while he raked the rose-beds. It was hot, and she wandered off to sit under the low branches of the frangipani tree, surrounded by sweet-smelling fallen flowers the colour of ice-cream. Sun filtered through in fractured geometric patterns, and she had been gazing at it for some time before she saw it. It clung immobile to a branch of the frangipani tree, its skin the colour of bark dappled with light and shade. Only its tongue flickered occasionally, darting out long and straight and with deadly accuracy, recoiling like a spring, some hapless insect in its toils. Magnified a thousand times, it could have been a dinosaur, except that, sitting there so innocuously in its bark-coloured skin, it seemed less animal than an organic part of the vegetable world it inhabited. It could have been another outgrowth of the tree, whose rough trunk sprouted knobs and whorls in profusion. Slender branches held aloft powerfully perfumed delicate satin flowers, each one perfect and separate, so you longed to pluck one just to possess it. Even if your hair was short and straight, a frangipani would sit behind your ear and lend you its beauty without drooping, like hibiscus, or falling apart, like flame tree petals. The chameleon had that strangeness and perfection about it too. Its tail, coiled like a tendril of mountain fern, was longer than its body. Clawed like a lizard, it balanced on its splayed toes with the delicacy of a fastidious lady in a fairytale confronted by an ugly suitor. For long moments, the swivelling of its large bulbous eyes was the only perceptible movement. When, almost hesitantly, it rocked forward, its motion was closer to a hover than a step.

The child, watching, was entranced. To her, it was a dragon, a mythical creature which had materialised in this garden out of a story only half-believed, as evidence of another order of being. 'They change colour,' the mother had once explained, 'so predators can't see them.' Any colour, the child wondered. Purple, like jacaranda? Yellow and red, like the too-sweet blossoms in the hedge? Green, like cactus? The creature looked so at home in its sun-dappled bark-skin, she couldn't imagine it flower-bright. Ask Ahmed. When she called his name, he appeared round the side of the house and she pulled him over to the tree. When he saw the chameleon he retreated abruptly several yards away. Rainbows danced in the child's eyes as she asked him, 'Ahmed, can it be blue? Can it be red?' Watching her, he was cool, holding himself aloof, eyes shielding themselves from the sun with a slight scowl. Between the two of them there was an easy friendship. She was too young yet to be a memsahib, and he was scarcely older than a child himself, had a sister her age. He liked to show off his knowledge of the garden, frighten her with snakes and centipedes. She always forgave him, for the sake of the world he opened to her. 'Can it, Ahmed? Can it?' 'Sijui,' he said curtly, and withdrew to the hose-pipe, and the technicalities of window-boxes. Often he let her help, gave her little things to do, and so she followed him, hurt but disbelieving. Abruptly, he turned his back and busied himself with the plant boxes on the verandah. He had taken refuge in work, where she couldn't follow, shutting her out, and she didn't know why. Blood rushed to her face and her eyes stung. She darted across the verandah, and was enfolded in the cool gloom inside the house.

Mariamu was in the kitchen, preparing vegetables for the family dinner. She moved rhythmically between the wooden table-top and the sink, wielding her knife with practised ease.

Mariamu was part of the child's world, like Ahmed. But because she was a grownup, she knew more than Ahmed, and the child relied on her when unconvinced by other people's versions of reality. So now she hung by the door, still flushed with that unnameable heat, and waited for Mariamu to notice her.

Humming a hymn tune just under her breath, Mariamu was engrossed, and it took her a few moments to register the child's presence. When at last she looked up, a smile instantly lit her face. 'Come and drink cold water and sit down. It's too hot for you outside,' she invited. Looking more closely, her smile gave way to concern. 'What's the matter?' she asked, seeing the child was close to tears.

'Ahmed.'

'What did Ahmed do to you?'

'Nothing.'

'Then why are you crying?'

'The chameleon. We found a chameleon.'

'And so? Why did that make you cry?'

The child shuffled, uncomfortably. She didn't know what she should say, or even if Ahmed had in fact done anything wrong. But Mariamu, in the cast-off dress with the faded wrapper over it, looked familiar and safe. She had no secrets from Mariamu, not even when she wet the bed after a bad dream and hid the sheet from her mother.

'He didn't want to tell me.'

'Tell you what?'

'About the chameleon. He knows, but he said he didn't.'

'Is that all?' the woman responded with a laugh. I'll tell you then. It's a story. Are you ready?'

The child settled herself on a stool at the wooden table and lifted her face in anticipation.

'Long ago,' said Mariamu, 'when God made the world, everyone was black. It didn't matter where you came from, everyone was the same colour, and it was black. Then he made

19

a pool for all the people to wash, and he called all the animals and sent them out to tell people to come. The cheetah is the fastest animal, and that one he sent to the white people. He sent the lion to the yellow people, the elephant to the brown people, and they all came and washed. The animal he sent to call the black people was the chameleon. It was so slow; by the time the black people came to the pool, there was hardly any water left. All they could do was stand in the puddle and bend over and place their palms flat in it. So that's why the only part of black people which is white is the palms of their hands and the soles of their feet. And that's why we hate the chameleon, because he cheated us.'

Mariamu had finished her peeling and slicing and was scooping skins and seeds into the metal jerrycan under the sink. The child sat still, taking in the story. She hadn't known black people didn't like being black. The black people she knew loved her, and she had never thought to question how they felt about themselves. They worked in the house or the garden or at her father's office, and seemed happy, just as she herself was happy. The story had cast a shadow where before there was only light. The story, or was it the chameleon? The chameleon, then, was not a fabulous beast in a fairytale, it was a real creature that brought bad luck. Was that why Ahmed had been cross? Not with her, but with the chameleon? As she struggled to make sense of his reaction, her mother's explanation for the creature's magical properties came back to her, and with it an idea. With a rush of excitement, she jumped off the stool. Mariamu, bent over, didn't see her leave the room.

Ahmed was no longer on the verandah, but a glance at the sun told her where to find him. She followed the familiar route, round the back of the garage where her parents' car rested at night, past the mulberry bushes she loved to plunder, to the servants' quarters. There were two rooms, Mariamu's and Ahmed's, and she was intimate with both. She knew the picture of the Virgin Mary over Mariamu's bed to which she prayed, and the pretty beads of the rosary that sat on a box by the bed. She knew the picture of Ann-Rose, now at a convent school in town, the rough feel of the blanket, the smell after the room had been closed up for a few hours while Mariamu was at work or at church. She knew the corner where Ahmed kept his schoolbooks, the smell of the paraffin lamp he studied by, the tattered black and white snapshot of his family, all eight of them. Next to the bedrooms was a small roofed area with an open entrance, which was their kitchen. She found Ahmed there, crouched by the cooking fire, fanning the embers under a blackened pot of water. Without waiting for him to see her, 'Ahmed,' she said in a rush, 'Mariamu told me why you don't like the chameleon, but it could also be your friend. It could show you how to change your colour. It's sorry for being so slow you didn't get to the pool in time. But you can be any colour you like. You don't have to be black.'

The boy continued his work of fanning the embers, waving a folded sheet of newspaper to and fro until the fire caught. Next he took the bag of maizemeal from the shelf, and set it carefully beside the pot while he waited for the water to boil. Then he reached over to the small cupboard where he and Mariamu kept their utensils, and selected the long wooden spoon, worn almost to a stick with turning. A meat-safe stood in a corner, a wooden frame with wire mesh tacked on to keep out flies, and four feet which stood in old condensed milk cans filled with water, to prevent the ants from climbing up. The child knew without looking that inside it was a small saucepan with the remnants of last night's stewed meat and gravy, waiting for its turn on the fire, and her mouth watered. Ahmed said nothing, but his movements were deliberate and precise, as though each gesture meant more than he could express in words. He was aware of the child's presence behind him, her shining expectancy. She loved the ugali and stew they ate with their fingers from the same bowl, would skip her food at home in the hope of being offered it. Normally, when she came at meal-times, he would invite her to eat. But today was different, in a way he could not explain to himself, much less to her. He had had to leave school and go out to work to help support his brothers and sisters. They were a long way away and he missed them, but the hours spent in the garden with her made his work like play. At those times, he would forget his loneliness and allow himself to be a child again. Now he was confused, and his confusion troubled him. It felt like a betrayal, but whose betrayal was it? He turned slightly, and regarded her over his shoulder. For a long moment he looked at the master's child standing on the threshold of his kitchen. He thought, *But after all, she is not my sister*, and his voice came suddenly, with unexpected harshness. 'Go away,' he said, and very gently, he poured the maizemeal into the bubbling water.

The child stepped back from the door and ran away. She sat for a long time under the mulberry bushes, which were low and uncomfortable but where she knew she wouldn't be found. She was breathing hard and could feel the heat rising from the bare earth all around her. Gradually, her breath slowed and a thought coalesced in her mind. The chameleon was the reason, it brought bad luck. She got up and went to the garage, where there was a pile of bricks left over from when they built the bombola, the wood-fired water-heater. She picked up one of them and walked steadfastly towards the frangipani tree. The sun had shifted since she was there before, and the geometry of light and shade had altered, as if a kaleidoscope had clicked once and all the pieces had fallen into a different pattern. She ducked under the branches and looked for the chameleon. Her eyes ran along the bark, alert to its disguise, willing it to appear. It moved so slowly, it was impossible it could have disappeared so soon. Seeing nothing, she climbed into the branches, higher and higher, until she could go no further, and in frustration she shook the tree so that more ice-cream flowers tumbled to the ground. Then she sat quietly, thinking. Gradually, the chameleon, Ahmed's reaction, Mariamu's story, her mother's explanation, all seemed to be of a piece. It was a fabulous beast inhabiting the real world, and they were right to be afraid of it. She was glad she hadn't killed it, and grateful to it for vanishing. If it was magic, it knew how she was feeling, and this was its answer. She heard tyres crunching on the gravel of the drive, and knew that soon someone would call for her. She dug in her claws and swayed slowly. High up in the frangipani tree, she too was invisible.

MARIAMU AND THE DEMON

Where did she come from? How old was she? Mariamu looked after me and my sisters from when I was very small, but I have only a handful of facts to play with. She was a Catholic (had she been to mission school?); she had a young daughter, Ann-Rose – there was no sign of a husband; she was gentle to the point of ineffectiveness; she used to call after the twins 'Alikizandra', or 'Wamary', as if they were a tribal group all of their own, and they would run away without answering; she was generous and allowed me to eat with her in her room in the servants' quarters, food she had paid for. She was always there; then one day, she wasn't. She joined TANU in the run-up to Uhuru and started going to night school; then she left, saying it wasn't right to work for white people. She had been with us as long as I could remember. I was three when we came to Moshi, but I associate her most with the house in Rombo Avenue opposite the tall white house on stilts that belonged to the doctor's family. So I must have been five or six. She was there at Uhuru, the year my last sister was born, when I was ten. She was still there when I was thirteen and sprouting breasts. Was it really less than ten years she was with us?

There was an aura of sadness and vulnerability about her. How common could it have been to have to bring up a child on your own? Would the church have condemned her for having a baby out of wedlock? Was that why she had to go and work for white people? Where were her family? What was it like for her, living so close to strange men in the servants' quarters? People she didn't know anything about, who she'd never met before they turned up there? People with a different religion, or who drank and made a noise sometimes.

And what about us, how did she feel about us, when we were kind to her, when we abused her? What was it like for her, looking after other people's children, during that time before Ann-Rose came to live with her? We communicated in Swahili, but how effective was that as a language I'd picked up from the garden-boy? She went to learn English at one point. She aspired to bettering herself. She must have had dreams, ambitions. Though to me she was a grownup, I realize now that she was young. She could have been in her twenties when she came, in her thirties when she left. She had a whole life after us of which I know absolutely nothing.

I remember her carrying my youngest sister on her back and singing. She must have carried the twins like that, too, whichever one wasn't with my mother at the time. She probably never carried me; I would have been too big already. The thought makes me jealous. I remember her hands washing me in the bath. I can see her standing in the kitchen, squeezing oranges. I used to hang around her and ask questions, and we would talk. I feel if I could only remember those conversations, I would have the key to something, but all that comes back is an atmosphere, a sense of connection, a sharing of secrets. I know I loved Mariamu. Even now, when I think of her, I can feel what she meant to me. But the memory is complicated: need, expectation, affection, admiration, separation, desertion, betrayal. I was a colonial child, she was my ayah, my parents' employee. There must always have been a distance between us, even if I was unconscious of it. But she would have known that though she took responsibility for us, played with us, achieved a depth of intimacy with us, we were not her children, and she could be let go at any moment.

Mariamu's room is dark and always shuttered when she's out. If she's in, she flings the window open to let in the light, and you can see her things. There's a picture of the Virgin holding her baby above the bed. It's all gold and blue and the most beautiful thing I have ever seen. Apart from the bed, there is no other furniture. Pots and pans stand in a neat row on the floor, with enamel bowls and a few battered spoons. Everything is very clean. There is a wooden box by the bed on which rests a bible, and a nail on the wall for clothes. The details of her room are familiar to me, and in that sense ordinary. Next to the room is a small kitchen, where she cooks on an open fire surrounded by bricks. Although there's a chimney, the walls are black with soot. When she blows on the wood to make it burn, smoke fills the room and she wafts it away with a fan of newspaper. The meals she cooks on this stove and shares with me are delicious. She cooks a sauce with small pieces of meat, and steamed maize meal which we call posho. I don't know why; the Swahili word is ugali. The food has a special smell, slightly smoky, strong, fragrant, starchy and meaty at the same time. We eat sitting on the ground, the steaming mound of posho and the small enamel dish of meat and gravy between us, breaking off bits of posho and dipping it in the sauce. The concrete is hard and scratchy beneath my thighs as I lean forward to dip, and when I've finished, I scrape bits of posho out from under my finger-nails, and suck the gravy off my wrist.

Of course, I took it for granted it was my right to do these things, to visit Mariamu in her room, to share her food, to ask her questions. I see now that the easy way she had of sharing was a gift that she bestowed on me. But if it was a gift, it was one whose value I only understood years after she herself had vanished from my life. Was I a spoilt child, overindulged and unappreciative? I know my father thought so, because he often complained about how we were waited on, and once decreed we should start to make our own beds. As we got older, and increasingly refused to fall in with his plans, he used to call us 'a graceless bunch'. This puzzles me now, because if he cared so much about gratitude, how come we took so many things for granted?

My conversations with Mariamu, I now realize, were surreptitious. They took place when my mother was elsewhere, busy, inattentive; when my father was at work, or playing tennis at the club, or buried in a book, or talking to my mother. We talked at intimate moments: brushing teeth, in the bath, getting dressed, or in her hot little room in the soporific afternoons, or at night in the half-lit living room while she baby-sat. We talked in Swahili, a language I no longer speak, though when I hear it, I understand what's being said. Swahili is like a secret imprinted in my brain to which I've lost the code. Mariamu's voice comes to me, muffled by time and distance, and speaking in code. But certain things stand out with startling clarity, moments which have retained a shape as solid as saucepans, an atmosphere as pungent as the woodsmoke from the bath heater at the back of the house: the time she told me the chameleon story, a parable which I finally understand; the time she taught me that there were different ways of viewing the world, and mine wasn't necessarily the right one.

Adolescence is an awkward time. I can feel my mother's eyes on me, watching me grow. She watches me with a mixture of anxiety and pride, which makes me defensive and shy. I know she's waiting for me to deliver something, but I don't know what. It's the early 60s, and in another part of the world, teenagers have been invented. Older children come back from boarding schools in England or Nairobi, wearing jeans and full skirts with pinched in waists. They bring the latest records, which we play on a portable turntable:

Got to please her
just cos she's a

27

living doll.
Take a look at her hair
it's real
if you don't believe what I say
just feel.

The tiny lumps swelling on my chest are uneven in size. When I walk anywhere, my sisters huddle together and giggle behind my back, and I struggle to fill a bra as a way of hiding what's happening. Thoroughly miserable, I complain to Mariamu, who laughs. 'That's how it is,' she says. 'One grows, then the other one grows, and in the end they're the same.' We're in the bathroom, standing by the mirror side by side. I'm naked, gazing disconsolately at my imperfections. She, as always, is wearing her blue uniform, with a starched white cap like a nurse's headdress. Her face in the mirror, on a level with mine, is swamped under the pointed cap, and she's thin in the too-big uniform. I'm as tall as she is, and still growing. We measure ourselves, back to back, waiting for when I will overtake her. I imagine she is saving money out of her wages to send to Ann-Rose, wherever she is. But she is still sharing her food with me.

Other things happened as I grew towards adolescence. I became more rebellious and more difficult to handle. There were frequent storms of tears, choking sobs and going off on my own to look for refuge. My father, an old-fashioned disciplinarian, was bemused by displays of feminine emotion, and my mother had to do a lot of mediating. On my side, I decided that I hated him, which made my mother very unhappy and that gave me satisfaction too. My sisters were a torment, noticing everything and passing comment so that I couldn't hide or pretend. Mariamu went on being her gentle, forbearing self, and with her I felt I could also be myself, whoever that was. She accepted my tempers and moods as inevitable and never judged, interrogated, or criticized. If she registered any reaction to my turbulence, it was amusement. Except for one indelible moment of dissent.

I don't remember the details of the conflict, but I imagine it was with my father. It usually was. Between my mother and me there was an unspoken understanding that, in his absence, many rules were relaxed. I slept in her bed when he was away, I sat with her at night and read to her, I stood by her dressing table and watched her do her hair and apply her make-up. And she talked to me, confiding things to me that make me feel grownup and important. At those times, I had a glimmering of how it might be to be a woman. When my father returned from safari, I reverted to being a child, sleeping with my sisters and going to bed instead of reading aloud. This arrangement worked for a while, until the breast problem came along, and a demon seemed to take up residence inside me. Suddenly I found it unbearable, insupportable, to be relegated. I felt I had more right to my mother's attention than he did. I had changed in ways he couldn't see and didn't understand, and he was the one being left behind. In this situation, there was a lot of potential for conflict.

Let's suppose it happened like this.

I want to go out, possibly to a film he deems unsuitable. A friend is going with her mother and I'm invited. 'You're not watching rubbish like that,' he says, with a full stop at the end of his voice. My mother's face looks sad and sympathetic, and left alone, she might talk him into it. 'Come on Jack, it's really not that bad. She's a big girl you know, and Susan's going.' But the demon rises up and snorts through my nostrils, spitting fire and brimstone. 'You never let me do anything I want! All my friends can go out when they want to! I hate you!' and so on. All my father can see is an insolent little girl who wants her own way. I can't say if he slaps me this time, though he has more than once when driven to it. But almost worse is when he puts on a stony expression and his lips become a hard thin line. My heat is no match for his cold, and it's I who am scalded by my own anger.

In a mood like this, I might fling away into another part of the house, banging the swing door with mosquito netting that separates the bedrooms from the living area. I might storm and rage for half an hour, and my mother would come and try to comfort me, and quite possibly give up if the demon really has a grip. Eventually, I calm down. The house is quiet, people going about their business regardless of my private drama. Then Mariamu's knock on the door, her gentle voice, the rustle of that ridiculous starched uniform. 'How are you? Do you feel better? Would you like some water?' Her arms around me and her laugh invite me to rejoin the world of the living. Normally, the demon would slink, defeated, back to its lair, and I'd get up and go with her to the kitchen and let her pour me a glass of cold water from the Gordon's Gin bottle in the refrigerator. But today, it still lurks, lashing its tail. 'Bring me the water here,' I say, not bothering to add please or look at her. Mariamu hovers, and tries again. She knows she has to coax me out of the bedroom or I'll sit there festering until I have a headache. Probably my mother has even told her to go and bring me out, and maybe I'm using that against her too. 'Come to the kitchen,' she urges, 'I have work to do and you can help me.' 'Helping' Mariamu is a privilege I usually leap at, as often I'm forbidden to distract her when she's working. But today I want to inflict as much damage as I can, and I turn my face cold like my father's, and say in his voice: 'Bring me the water here.' Mariamu is nonplussed, I can tell from her silence. And then comes the last spurt of hellfire from the subsiding fury, and I say the thing that has haunted me through the decades since she disappeared. 'Do what I say. You have to do what I say, because you're black and I'm white.'

Mariamu doesn't speak, but the air in the room goes cold

and clammy. I can feel the sweat on my face and hands, and hear my breath. I still haven't looked at her, and now I don't dare. We stay like that, me feeling her eyes on me but not daring to look, for what feels like eternity. At last I hear her sigh, and rustle. When she speaks, it's so softly I have to strain to catch it. 'Little sister,' she says, and the sadness in her voice lacerates me worse than my father's hardness or my own outrage. 'God made white and black and he made them the same. When you want me, you'll find me in the kitchen.' I hear the shoosh of her bare feet on the concrete, the click of the door. I am alone, facing myself.

By the time Mariamu left us, the breast problem was more or less resolved and they were as near the same size as they would ever be. For a long time, we didn't know where she was or what she was doing. Then one day my sisters and I were in town with my mother, and we went to the Livingstone Hotel for cokes and coffee. It wasn't called the Livingstone any more by then, it had changed after Uhuru to the KNCU (and gone downhill, people said). A group of women were cleaning at the other end of the long dining room, talking and clattering buckets and brooms. Suddenly, one of the women detached herself, and flung herself at my mother, exclaiming with joy. With a shock, I recognized Mariamu. She had changed, was more vibrant than I ever remembered, her eyes shining, her face filled out. She seemed possessed of a new confidence, as if in shedding her ayah's uniform and passing out into the world she had become someone else. Who she had become was a mystery, and has remained so. I was shy and awkward, but she was almost ebullient, asking my mother questions and laughing the high-pitched joyful laugh I remembered from many, many private jokes shared only with me.

That was the last time I saw Mariamu. After that one reappearance, it was as if she evanesced. I know she left me with the answers to many questions imprinted in my brain, but in that indecipherable code. I used to think of her as having disappeared from my life, but now I think that it was the other way round – I disappeared from hers. It was me who evanesced, and this existence I'm experiencing is all a dream of Mariamu's.

MARANGU

It was hot and dry and everyone was irritable, including the dog. He lay panting on the shrivelled grass in the shade cast by the wall of the house, or soothed his belly on the cool concrete floor of the living room. Every so often, he snapped his jaws as a fly buzzed his head, and saliva flew in all directions.

The children played in a welter of swimsuits and tackies, while their mother screwed down the thermos full of hot tea and wrapped the banana and marmite sandwiches in wax paper. The car stood in the driveway, all its doors open, and the father came and went, stowing things – a blanket for sitting on, the picnic basket, the bag of towels – before calling them to climb in. They were going to Marangu, to get some relief from the heat. The dog looked dolefully after the departing car before settling back into a half-doze on the verandah.

Marangu was a special treat, and the children sat excitedly in the back of the car, not minding that their bare legs stuck to the seat or sweat broke out as soon as someone touched your skin. As they left town, the breeze blew red dust into their eyes and played havoc with the mother's hair, but nobody complained. They sat forward to see who would be the first to spot the ancient baobab which marked the turn-off, so vast that an entire family couldn't get their arms around it.

The eldest girl saw it first, the spindly branches sprouting from the great solid trunk. It was a magic tree uprooted by God and made to grow upside down with its roots in the air for daring to complain about something. What did it complain about? She couldn't remember, but it seemed a fitting punishment for a tree. A tree that size would be at least five hundred years old, her father had told her. Five hundred years of growing upside down, its branches buried in the ground, unable to see. You could live off its bark and the water it contained if you were lost in the savannah, but she never had been. And people were buried in the trunk sometimes, so spirits lived in it. Tree of life and death, she thought, like in the Bible. Or was it good and evil?

After the tree, the car turned left off the main road and started to climb. The air became clearer, caressing your face instead of rasping at it, carrying the faintest hint of moisture to revive you after the dust and drought lower down. They were ascending the mountain, drawing closer and closer to its secret self, and the closer they drew, the more the mountain changed. In the town where they lived, the mountain was a far white peak shrouded in cloud, emerging suddenly at evening, shining and afloat on its raft of white. Marangu was a village on the lower slopes of the mountain, surrounded by little shambas of bananas and coffee. In Marangu, the mountain peak, when it emerged, seemed lower, almost at eye-level. The drama of distance was replaced by intimacy of connection, so that the elements , earth, air, water, were redolent of the mountain – earth dark, rich and fertile, air cool and thin, water cold and sparkling like liquid sunlight.

They left the car and scrambled down the hillside to the picnic spot by the river, the favourite spot they had made their own. It was a flat, green space of riverbank, where you could throw down the rug and set up the thermos as you struggled into your swimsuit. The river called to the children and they couldn't wait to immerse themselves in it, cold as it was. It came straight from the mountain, from a glacier which dissolved as it descended, so cold it burnt your skin when you dived in. You stood on a rock, dipped in a toe and recoiled shrieking, but you couldn't resist, you must be in that water and you slid off the rock and let the current take you, bumping against rocks and laughing with high-pitched hysteria at the freezing shock. The parents, glad of a few moments of peace, lay on the bank and breathed the air, inhaling its freshness.

Later, they ate the sandwiches and digestive biscuits, and lay about reading. The children played on the rocks, and the girl found herself at a little distance, wandering along the river bank. On the other side, she could see a cloud of bright butterflies hovering like brilliant dust-motes above a carpet of purple flowers. She stopped to look, stepping onto a stone in the river. It became suddenly very quiet, as if all the noise had drained away and instead, colours thrust themselves at her. In the distance, the scarlet bells of an African flame tree seared the air. Flat brown rocks lay tumbled in the river, humped and smooth like the glossy backs of hippos, half-submerged in the black and silver water. And all around green, green. She began to pick her way from rock to rock, winding slowly upstream. After a while, she became aware of a sound, a continuous rushing, which grew louder as she went on. She was unable to stop, or turn around, the sound drew her and she went forward as if hypnotized, blind and deaf to everything but the colours and sound of the river.

The noise is suddenly very loud. It fills her ears like the ringing of bells, and she finds herself, without warning, at the foot of a sheet of white water, pouring itself over the edge of a black rock face. It is immensely tall, so that it seems to her as if the water pours from a hole in the sky itself, and she sits down hard with shock on the rock beneath her. She stays very still, barely breathing. The water seems to race forward and hurl itself over the edge, dashing itself into a million sparkling shards on the rocks below, then flinging itself high, high in the air, covering her skin in tiny glittering drops. The water is so white against the black rock, she thinks of colobus monkeys with their long black hair with its flash of white, leaping through the trees. After some time, she becomes aware that she is in a great gorge of sculpted rock, like the rocks in her mother's book of old paintings, with pilgrims wending their way on horseback. At either side, white trumpet lilies extend their prayerful hands from the banks, framing the waterfall. She thinks of the lilies in the painting of the Virgin on the wall in Mariamu's room. She sits a long time on the rock in the river gazing at the waterfall, caressed by its shattered droplets, over-whelmed by the animal roar of its crashing and splintering. She is outside of time, outside even of herself. Nothing exists except the endless transformation of the white water pouring itself ceaselessly over the black rock, from ice, to water, glass, spray, vapour, glitter, droplets, monkey-tail, lion-roar.

When she came to, terror rushed in to fill the vacuum. While she sat, the darkness had gathered around her, and she turned and hurried back, slipping on wet stones, seeking the sunlight. Almost sobbing in her haste, she saw in passing an old man standing stock still on the riverbank. She saw his tattered shorts, nondescript, discoloured shirt, and the battered tin bucket at his feet in a blur as she rushed past. She felt his eyes on her but was already leaping for the other bank, running towards the picnic spot and her parents.

They were standing in a rigid group, two adults, two children, faces turned towards her. The rug was folded at her mother's feet, the picnic basket next to it, the towels back in the bag. She stopped abruptly a few feet away, panting, her face red, her eyes full of tears. She saw her father make an irritable gesture, but before he could say anything, her mother stepped forward.

'There you are! We didn't know where you'd got to. It's time to go home.'

'Where were you? Why didn't you let us come?'

'You're very lucky this is Chagga country. An old farmer passed by and said he'd seen you at the waterfall. He said you were coming back so we waited.'

'He told us a story about it! It's called Ndoro, that's Colobus in kiChagga…'

'He said a young girl from Marangu got pregnant and went there to kill herself because she wasn't married…'

'…And a leopard came when she was standing right at the top of the waterfall, and startled her, and she fell into the water and was killed.'

'We thought a leopard might have got you!'

'We want to see the waterfall too!'

'Next time; it's too late today. Look, it's getting dark already.'

'Come on girls, get the stuff into the car and we'll stop for a drink on the way home.'

The girl held her mother's hand as they walked back to the car, too full of her secret to speak. They stopped at a bar on the side of the road and drank Coca Cola, dark and sweet with a white foam when it was poured, and she thought of the white spray and the black rock, the girl falling headlong, the bubbles rising, the leopard, the old man. She wanted to tell them, but she couldn't find the words.

'ALMOST LIKE ENGLAND'

On the way to the station, she sat in the back holding her mother's hand. The ring on her mother's finger had a green stone, with little white stones on either side. The green stone was called an emerald, and it matched her dress. Her mother's hand was soft and the nails had little white half moons. She looked at them all the way till they arrived at the station, wondering if she should tell about the dirty knickers she'd dropped behind the bookcase. You weren't supposed to have accidents at eight years old. The small platform was crowded with children going to school and parents who had come to see them off. She said hello to Susan, who was clinging to her mother. Together, they watched as their suitcases were loaded in the luggage van and found seats together on the train. Their parents stood in a group on the platform, talking and waving, and they stood by the window and waved back. Then the engine began to puff, slowly at first, then faster and faster, and with the first jolt of the train she saw her mother's green dress detach itself from the group as she ran towards the window and grabbed her hand. As the train moved slowly out of the station, her mother ran alongside, holding her hand through the window, till the platform ended and she let go. Looking back, the child saw the green dress standing by itself, and then the train hooted and the dress was lost in a cloud of white smoke.

She and Susan compared their packed suppers. Hers had banana and honey sandwiches, crisps and a bar of Cadbury's. It was a little bit exciting, being on a train without their parents, and they played snap together in the space between them and talked about leaving home. At bed-time, a man in a uniform came and undid some straps behind them to let down the top bunk, and Susan agreed she could have it. You had to climb up a little ladder attached to the side, and up there you were close to the ceiling and had a light all of your own. You could see the track between the carriages when you went to the bathroom, and the lavatory bowl was bottomless, with the ground rushing by underneath. Do not use the toilet while the train is standing at the station. EAR & H. That meant East African Railways and Harbours; her father had said so. During the long night she lay awake and the train chugged on and on through the darkness. She had no idea how far they had to go, no concept of distance at all. She was travelling blind, praying that she would know what was expected of her when she got there. The wheels made a rhythm as they passed over the wooden sleepers, plunkety plunk whoosh plunkety plunk whoosh, carrying her further and further from home.

Very early, the train stopped at Mombo station, and they all got off. It was cold, and mosquitoes etched the blue-black air with their whining. She lined up with the other children who were being shepherded onto a big bus in the station courtyard, feeling sleepy and stiff. She knew the school was in the mountains; her mother had told her so. (Beautiful climate, much cooler. Almost like England.) Soon after they left Mombo, the bus began to grind and churn its way uphill, lurching round hairpin bends and swaying sickeningly from side to side. Diesel fumes belched from the exhaust and infiltrated eyes and lungs, filling stomachs already queasy from the mountain road. The plains were a long way behind; who knew what lay ahead?

The child sat in the bus, paralysed with nerves and nearly asphyxiated by diesel. She both wanted and didn't want to be sick. The prospect of confessing, of stopping the bus and getting out in full view of everyone, was too much for her. She was used to being car-sick on long journeys. Her father would stop the car and she and her mother would get out, and her mother would hold her forehead. Afterwards, she would give her cold water from the thermos flask, and wipe her face with a damp cloth. Without the comfort of this ritual, the child did not dare to be sick, so she struggled with the nausea in silence, holding down her fear in a hard knot at the pit of her stomach. The effort made her pale, and bathed her in a cold sweat. Her mother's warmth was a day-old memory, along with home and everything safe and familiar. For the first time in her life, she was alone, and every muscle in her body was tense with concentrating on what this meant.

At the end of the journey, there would be school. She wondered what it would be like. Till now, school had been just up the road from home, and she had walked there in the morning with Mariamu in her purple and white checked uniform and her Clark's shoes and white socks, and at lunch-time, her father had picked her up and taken her home. No-one had told her school could be a big room with long wooden tables and hard benches and lumpy porridge with unwinnowed seeds still in it. Tea so sweet you choked. Bells and silence, shared baths and beds in rows in a dark room where you were not supposed to talk and children wept separately at night. No-one to kiss you when the light went out. A fat matron who sent you to fetch a slipper and whacked you in front of everyone if you did something wrong. Letters home on Sundays, which the teacher read afterwards to check the spelling. She did not know what to write, but the teacher said she had to. So she wrote:

Dear Mummy and Daddy, I arrived safely. I am in Form One with Miss Wilson. French is hard. We had hockey and I was left wing. The film on Saturday was Ice-cold in Alex. It was good. Please could you send me a new hairbrush. I forgot mine on the train. How are Mariamu and Ann-Rose and Ahmed, and the guinea pigs and ducklings and Sebastian? Has he bitten anyone else? Give my love to the twins. Tell them they are lucky to be at home.

She couldn't think of her mother without tears, and she drooped her head to hide them. Mummy Mummy, at night I am cold but I keep the empty box of face-powder under my pillow and take it out and sniff, and pretend my face is buried on your knees while I say my prayers. I hold the pudding in my mouth until I can get downstairs and spit it out in the lavatory bowl. I hate the grey shorts, they're too tight and my bottom sticks out. I have to go backwards through the door so people don't laugh at me. A rat got into my suitcase and ate the paper my shoes were wrapped in and Miss Livingstone was cross with me. I didn't know. How long till I come home?

The child hung her head and tears dripped onto her hands as the teacher read her letter, marking the mistakes with a pencil.

At her writing desk in the living room, the woman folded the letter she had written. There was another letter she could have written, but the child was only eight years old and the time for that letter had not arrived. Meanwhile, she knew what was required.

> My darling,
> I hope you arrived safely and are settling down. We all miss you very much, but it's only five weeks and two days till half-term. Daddy says we can stay at the lodge in the forestry project up there. He has written to his friends in Lushoto to ask them to take you out. You are allowed to go out one Saturday or Sunday each side of half-term.
> All the animals are fine and the ducklings have grown. What have you learnt to say in French? When

41

I come up, you'll have to speak some for me. I learnt it too in school, but I've forgotten most of it. You can teach me! Everyone asks after you and sends love, the twins are drawing pictures to send you with this letter. Ahmed is watering your plants and Mariamu prays for you. It won't be long, my darling. Try and eat the food and grow tall and strong.

Love from Mummy.

P.S. I saw the Larsens at the Club, and Anna said she wished she could go to boarding school!

She wrote the school address on the envelope and stood by the window, gazing at the scorched garden.

I've cried every day since you went away. When we saw you off at the station, I had to pretend I was all right because I could see how terrified you were. I smiled and said how much fun to travel overnight on a train, and gave you your supper in a plastic bag, into which I had packed every treat I could think of, but I suspect you will have been too nervous to eat. All that went with you – your trunk, bedding and uniform, jars of jam and packets of sweets, presents from friends at home, envelopes already addressed for you to write home to us – reminded me how far you were going: 400 miles. The teacher was a nice, plump, youngish Englishwoman, and I felt a little better after I met her. But when I saw your face at the window, white with terror, something broke, and as the train gathered steam and started to move out of the station, I darted forward and clung to your hand through the window, running along the platform till it ended and our hands parted and your face merged with the clouds of white smoke. I watched the train till it was out of sight and then I had no choice but to turn and walk back.

I went home and sat on your bed and cried. Everything was in its place, your favourite bedtime stories, your collection of dolls, your dresses in the cupboard, your drawings on the blackboard. Only you were missing, and for twelve long weeks, I have to learn to live without you. Jack comforted me that it was a good school, the best in the territory, that the alternative was to send you to Kenya, or even home to England, that we'd see you when we came up for your half-term weekend, that there were other Moshi children at the school. I couldn't admit, even to him, that I was crying for myself, for that part of me you brought to life by being born.

I didn't know much about giving birth, but when the pains started, Jack and I climbed into the battered Bedford truck, and set off for Lindi hospital, 64 miles away. We bounced and jolted our way down 4000 feet of escarpment, to reach the dirt road which would take us to the coast. At first, I could ride the pains by gripping the truck door and holding on as hard as I could, because the gaps between were long enough. After a while, though, the pain and the jolting started to merge into one long sheet of agony, and Jack kept looking at my face and cracking jokes to keep me going. We were nearly there when we came to a point normally crossed by a small bridge. There was nothing there in the long dry season except a furrow which we had crossed dozens of times without even really noticing it. That day, the day you were born, it was the middle of the rainy season, and we came to a halt by a torrent of muddy reddish-brown water which rushed and gurgled across our path. The bridge had been washed away. Jack glanced at me and what he saw made him look grim, but all he said was, 'Don't worry, old girl, we'll get you there in time,' as he swung the steering wheel around and turned the truck back up the dirt road.

The detour took us an extra two hours, but I remember nothing except my longing to arrive. I wanted to get to that hospital more than I'd ever wanted anything in my life. I wanted the jolting and swaying to stop, I wanted clean sheets and a quiet room and nurses and someone to take the pain away. I didn't have a comforting self-help manual to take me through the stages, but when I felt the pressure building, building, I knew you were coming. It was like a fire in my pelvis, about to explode outwards and engulf me and every-thing near me. When the truck stopped, Jack, who knew even less than I did, helped me down from the passenger seat and into the small concrete building smelling of antiseptic. God,

44

they wanted me to climb the stairs. Between Jack and the wall, I inched my way up them, my body burning, my breath coming in moans. Halfway up, I collapsed on a step. I was actually sitting on your head. You came within minutes of our arrival in the room they took me to.

You, my first-born. Having you is the only one of life's experiences which has lived up to expectations. When I saw your damp brown head, your tiny fingers, I knew for certain life *could* fulfil its promises. Till that point, I had been waiting, neck eagerly outstretched like a fledgling waiting to be fed. When I was 18, and the war came, I joined the WRNS and found myself posted to Tanganyika. Young men I loved and danced with on shore were torpedoed at sea. I found that life went on. The war itself was built on a promise, which we fought for and many of us died for. Afterwards, my best friend from the war, a woman with the name of a flower, invited me to stay in her beautiful house in a quiet village in the English countryside. She had met and married a handsome doctor in India, and that same weekend, a childhood friend of her husband's came to stay. There was only one spare room. Instead of offering it to me, this other house-guest claimed priority, and I slept on the sofa. From this first meeting, I learnt never to expect him to do the conventional thing. Three weeks later, I was ironing a favourite blouse when the telephone rang and a voice like crushed velvet asked me to marry him. I forgot the blouse, and when I went back, the iron had burnt a hole in it.

Jack was six months younger than me and half an inch shorter. He sent his mother a telegram saying 'I'm marrying a woman who's taller, older and heavier than me'. He had been a fighter pilot in the RAF and was shot down and spent three years in prison camps in Italy and Germany, where he lived on cabbage stalks and fruit from the surrounding fields. He still looked like a scarecrow. After the marriage service, we stood on the steps of the church and I expected him to say – what? What

45

do men say to the women they have just married? He pointed to a tree in the churchyard and said, 'Look it's a' – and gave me a long Latin name. The picture of us on those church steps captures my astonished amusement. It set the tone for our marriage. If it didn't fulfil my expectations, it was because it simply dismantled them and put something else in their place.

After being confined for three years, Jack's only thought was to do something that would let him be free, out of doors, and self-directed. He retrained as a forester, joined the Colonial Service, and in 1949, I found myself back in Tanganyika, but this time upcountry, away from anywhere, with a ravine on one side and primeval forest on the other three sides. After the activity of the war years, the parties, the dances, the friendships, the working together for a common cause, it wasn't easy to be alone, just me and this man I'd married, in the wilderness, in Africa. But marriage was one of life's promises and I was there for its fulfilment, hoping to recognise IT when I saw it. Jack's job was to map the forest, 32,000 acres of it. The first year we were there, I walked over 300 miles with him, with porters and tents and a tin bath, a cook and provisions and kerosene lanterns, guns for protection against the animals, a precious bottle of whisky from which we had one glass each every evening. We slept in the bush, skirmished with lion and leopard and elephant, avoided poisonous snakes, and walked all day in single file. I washed my hair in the streams we passed, and forgot about make-up. It was a long way from Kensington, and any life I had known before, but it was an adventure that we shared. The alternative would have been to stay home, alone, in the house on the edge of the ravine, with its thatched roof full of scorpions and snakes and insects that fell on your plate as you were eating.

When I got pregnant, with you, in the second year, that is exactly what I did. I had the wireless and the BBC World Service, the Singer I had brought from home and books and books of poetry. I listened to the wheeze and crackle from Bush

House in London and pictured the Strand on a rainy day, and meeting a friend for lunch at Lyons. I read Tennyson and the Romantics and A.E Housman, and even wrote a few poems myself. I sewed clothes for you and dresses for me. My beautiful Liberty print dresses, bought in London before we left, were faded and worn from constant washing in rough soap and drying in the midday sun. Jack brought me cottons from the Indian dealers on the coast and I cut them out according to patterns that were already out of date. There were no regular trips to the gynaecologist to check weight and blood pressure, no friendly antenatal classes where you could meet other pregnant women and learn to breathe through labour. I knew I should eat healthily, but our food all had to be transported from the coast, and we lived mainly on tins. The monks at the Benedictine monastery 15 miles away grew vegetables, but eggs came from twice that distance. We ate fresh meat when we were able to shoot something, an antelope, every few weeks. We had no electricity, and it was hard to preserve things in the heat, with a refrigerator which ran on paraffin. Our water came by truck from the river 12 miles away, and we boiled it because of bilharzia.

We took you home and started to improvise caring for a baby. We had to keep your cradle covered at all times because of things dropping out of the roof. I wanted to put you outside in the sunshine, but Jack said you would be bait for the leopards. We built a lion and leopard-proof cage for you, and hired a small boy called Ali to sit and watch you and raise the alarm if anything came out of the forest. I breast-fed you as long as I could because there was no other milk, and when it was time to wean you, I started saving the bath water and dribbling it drop by drop onto tomato seedlings brought from the coast. I would pick and steam those tomatoes, and painstakingly sieve them for you, and you would fill your cheeks and spurt them across the room.

I was aware that I was lucky to be able to keep you alive at all.

Other women's babies on the Rondo Plateau were weaned at three months onto whatever everyone else was eating – mainly pounded maize meal and gravy – and left to survive as best they could. Many died before they reached two years old, of bilharzia, or malaria, or some ordinary childhood illness like measles. Or they could be eaten by animals which came out of the forest. The little dog which kept me company when Jack was away on safari was eaten by a leopard, right there in our garden. You survived.

And now you've gone away to school. So far away, you could be on the moon. The day you left, I don't know who was more nerve-ridden, you or me. You, at eight years old, going to face something you couldn't even imagine. Me, your mother, sending you away, out of my reach, into someone else's care. Someone who couldn't love you as I did, who wouldn't know how to interpret your expressions as I did, while I was left at home, feeling helpless, redundant. I had to pretend to be brave because I was a grownup. You also pretended to be brave, but after you left, the house-boy brought me a pair of nerve-soiled knickers you had felt too ashamed to confess to. He found them behind the bookcase, where you had dropped them. Did you set off knickerless into that unknown world? What have I sent you to, and how will you find your way without me?

MARIA MORPHOPOLOUS'S SLIPPER

The sun filtered through the branches and played on the silvery trunks of the young trees, releasing the sharp medicinal tang of eucalyptus. It tickled their noses and reached right down into their lungs, like inhaling Vicks when you have a cold. They were building a den in the bhundu, out of bounds. They were making it out of sticks stuck close together in the ground, wound through with the long grass that grew at the bhundu's edge. That part was hard, heaving it up in clumps without being seen by anyone on the playground. If they were caught they'd be in trouble, but the danger only made it more exciting.

There were three of them, and they had sworn an oath of secrecy. They could never divulge the other members of the gang, and they had to stay loyal to each other forever. It was hard to have secrets when you were always surrounded by other people, night and day, watched over even when you were asleep. But they had found ways to talk, whispering softly after lights-out, or finding a corner of the playground during play-time away from the others. The playground was big, it was like a small hill. Most people stayed at the bottom, where it was flat and you could run more easily. But if you climbed the hill you could disappear over the top, and hardly anyone went up there. You just had to be careful not to miss the bell when it went, calling you back to class.

There was a eucalyptus plantation right at the end of the playground, which they were forbidden to enter because they couldn't be seen. This was the bhundu, and it was where they were building the den. Now it was almost finished, and they were impatient to use it. Linnie went first, crawling through the low entrance, then Nita, then Jill. Inside, the air was close and fragrant, the smell of dried grass mingled with trampled earth, warm skin, matted hair, crumpled cotton. They sat with their knees drawn up, stooped over and facing each other, hidden. At first, the only noise was the sound of three girls breathing, then gradually you could hear the scuffle of ants in the eucalyptus bark, the chirruping of birds and, very faintly, the high pitched cries of children playing far away.

Nita fished a scrap of paper out of the pocket of her shorts, and a stump of pencil. It was time to sign the Pact. Leaning it against her knee she wrote: 'We, the Silent Three, do solemnly swear never to reveal each other's names and always to be faithful, loyal and true. Signed:' She wrote her name, and passed the paper to Jill, who passed it to Linnie. When they had all signed, they looked at each other in silence. Jill was the first to speak.

'We should bury it so no-one can find it.'

'But it'll rot in the ground.'

'Put it in a plastic bag?'

'Or in a secret place in the dorm.'

'What secret place? You know Potty sticks her nose in everything.'

'OK, but we haven't got a plastic bag.'

In the end, they agreed to take it back with them and hide it in the torn lining of Nita's overnight bag until they could bury it safely. But there was one more thing. Linnie said: 'We have to seal the Pact.' Two pairs of eyes looked at her expectantly. 'We have to *prove* it, don't you see? It's not enough just to promise, anyone can do that. We have to *do* something and not tell anyone about it.'

There was silence for a while, the grass wall tickling their backs, the warm smell enclosing them. The world seemed far away, as if they were in a capsule where time stood still and only closeness and secrecy mattered. When they crawled out at last, they were surprised by the brightness of sun on leaves, the harshness of the light. It seemed the day had moved on without them, and suddenly they panicked, running pell-mell through the trees and out onto the open slope of the hillside. A bell was ringing insistently, and they panted up the slope, cresting the hill, tumbling down the other side, to join the end of the queue of children disappearing towards the classrooms.

Seal the Pact. Prove it. Do something. The words chased each other through Jill's mind all through the afternoon. They were a challenge, a provocation. In bed after lights out, she stuck her head out of the mosquito net and leaned across the gap between her and Linnie to whisper: 'I know, let's go down to the river. Tell Nita.' She heard a rustle as Linnie leaned over, the susurration of breath. Without waiting, Jill crept out of bed, careful not to knock anything or wake anyone. There was a light at the far end of the corridor, enough to see her way to the head of the stairs. Silently, like a pyjamaed ghost, she flitted along the wall, till her bare feet found the first step. Below her the stairs were a dark well, leading away from safety. Unhesitatingly, she plunged into it, her toes curling around the edge of each step, her fingers trailing the wall, all her senses alert. At the bottom, complete darkness. She halted, hearing only the sound of a heart beat and shallow breathing, seeing nothing, smelling the rubber of flipflops and tackies, a faint whiff of soap left over from bath time. Gradually, shapes came into view: sports clothes hanging on pegs, basins under the window, shoe lockers. She moved forward cautiously, wondering for the first time if she was alone, or if anyone was coming to join her.

Jill folded herself onto a shoe locker, beneath a peg, arranging the smelly sports shirt so it fell like a curtain. She waited. Again, as in the den, she felt detached, suspended in a timeless space, but this time alone, without the comforting presence of the other two. A voice came out of the darkness, and she gave a little shriek: 'Linnie! You gave me such a fright! Where's Nita?' Linnie materialized in front of her, a small tousled head above rumpled pyjamas. Her eyes glittered, striking sparks off the cold white enamel of the basins. 'Sssh, silly, Potty'll hear us! Nita's too scared, she doesn't want to come. We'll give her a dare later. Let's go now.'

Unlatching the door was the easiest thing, and then they were outside. It was bright compared with inside, an upstairs window casting a square of yellow on the dirt driveway, a fragment of moon beginning to show through the clouds. They ran across the road towards the bank that fell away to the river, a place that was also out of bounds, a place they had only glimpsed from above in the day time, with African women washing the school sheets on the rocks below. As they flung themselves down the bank, it was as if their pyjamaed bodies took off, lifting into the air, impelled by the sheer joy of movement and held aloft by darkness. Together they floated to the bottom, and came to rest on the river bank. The moon was fully out now, striking the white trumpets of the lilies that grew there so they almost rang with the clarity of colour and light. Jill's eyes, when they sought Linnie's, saw mirrored back her own elation at the surge of flight that had carried them to where they stood. Their eyes reflected the moonlight off the lilies and the water, like nocturnal hunting creatures, alert and expectant of prey. Instinctively, they sought each other's hand, stepping onto the wide flat rock where the sheets were scrubbed, feeling the day's warmth rising through the soles of their bare feet. The water lapped at the rock, like a cat's tongue at a saucer. As if they could communicate just by touch, without a word spoken, they slipped out of their pyjamas and stepped in. The water was cool around their ankles, but as they stood there, it got warmer, and they went further, further, feeling it rise up their legs, surround their tummies, tickle their armpits. Their feet lifted and they were floating, two dark heads breaking the surface, their bodies pale and luminous beneath the water. From the reeds, a frog croaked, but otherwise it was silent. Above them loomed the massive outline of the school, with all the sleeping children, guarded by the sleeping matron. They lay on their backs, eyes filled with moonlight, holding hands.

'Nita, you have to seal the Pact.' They were back in the dorm, discussing the next step. 'You have to do something to show you're one of the Silent Three.' Nita hung her head, and her long black hair made a veil around her face. She wanted to be in the gang, to be one of a threesome with her two best friends, but she was used to being good. She didn't know how to break rules and lacked the recklessness of the other two. She was a girl in a family of many children, and girls played together in the house, or helped the women in the kitchen. It was boys who played outside, chasing balls into the neighbours' gardens, shouting and fighting and being rough. She could no more get out of bed after lights out and creep downstairs than she could fly. The den was one thing: it was daylight, and the bhundu was easy to get to, you just melted into the trees. But the river, at night… she shuddered.

They stood in a line outside the screen which protected the portable toilet. At night, if they needed to wee, that was where they had to go, not downstairs to the main bathrooms. The dormitories were on the first floor, giving onto alcoves which had large windows about thirty feet above the school driveway. The toilet was in one of these alcoves, its two windows standing open to let out the chemical smell. Jill and Linnie had dragged Nita out of bed, and stood one each side of her. Potty was safely in her room, the door closed, the radio playing. If she came out, all she would see was three little girls using the portable toilet, and the worst she could do was pack them off back to bed. They weren't breaking any rules.

'Go on,' said Linnie. 'You have to do it.' Nita wanted to move, but her limbs were frozen. She looked as if she would cry. 'I'll go first,' said Jill hurriedly, and climbed onto the window sill. It wasn't hard: lift your leg, step through the window, put your foot on the narrow ledge that ran along the outside of the building. Hold the window frame, bring the other leg outside, and now you're pressed flat against the wall, facing the brickwork, just room for your toes, your heels sticking out into thin air. Shuffle shuffle shuffle towards the other window, still holding on with one hand extended behind you. Then comes the moment when you have to let go, you're in the middle of the narrow ledge, you can't go back, you must go forward, shuffle shuffle shuffle, not looking down, don't think, just keep going keep going, till your fingers make contact with the other window frame, hold on, reach the window, lift one leg, climb over the ledge, bring the other leg in, and you're home. The second window was behind the toilet screen, so that even if someone passed, they couldn't see you climbing in. It was safe, it was the safest dare they could think of to seal the Pact.

It was Nita's turn. She turned blindly, facing the window. Watching her clamber awkwardly onto the sill, Jill felt a rush of anxiety. Nita wasn't good at games, she always dropped catches, she couldn't run fast, and mostly she preferred to sit on the sideline at hockey. Maybe she couldn't do it, maybe they were wrong to ask. But Nita was already lifting her leg over the sill, as delicate as a cat. Linnie stepped into the cubicle and leant through the second window. 'Come on Nita!' she urged. 'Just walk!' Nita clung to the window frame, trembling. Jill whispered, 'Go on, it isn't hard, honestly.' The long black hair fell across Nita's face, and she turned her head towards Linnie and the other window. Her narrow feet gripped the ledge as she took one tentative step sideways. 'Do it fast!' hissed Jill. You had to do it fast, it was the only way. If you stopped and looked down, if you stopped moving, you'd be stuck. Nita was doing it wrong, taking tiny little steps with long pauses in between when she seemed to freeze like a lizard against the wall. It took agonizing moments for her to shuffle out into the middle, to the point where her arm was fully extended behind her and she would have to let go. Then she stopped. 'Let go! You have to let go! Keep moving!' At the other window, Linnie was up on the sill and leaning towards her, arm outstretched. In a second, Nita could have touched her, gripped her hand, regained the safety of the second window frame. Jill saw her small, clenched fingers loosen as she lurched forward another step. Then, at the dead centre, she froze.

The face turned towards Linnie was pale and drenched with tears, the eyes wide with accusation. Below them, the ground beckoned and Linnie knew she had to do something. Without thinking, she lifted her leg and climbed out onto the sill, extending her arm so that her fingers touched Nita's, like figures in a frieze. At that moment, Jill heard a door open behind her and the rolling tread of a large body in soft shoes advancing towards the alcove. Miss Potgieter on her rounds! She couldn't get caught standing by the window, and in panic she turned and ran in the direction of the dormitory. Too late. The large, heavy flashlight Miss Potgieter always carried flicked on, and she was caught in its beam, exposed there in her pyjamas and bare feet, with all the consequences that must surely follow: interrogation, confession, punishment. Betrayal. What was she doing out of bed? Why was she running? Who else was with her? What were they up to? The cold, clipped authoritarian voice, the dead white hands gripping the flashlight like a weapon, the shadowy bulk behind it, all these would have to be endured while she squirmed, small, stupid, wrongful, rule-breaking, guilty, doomed to humiliation and certain pain.

But the important thing, they were far enough away from the toilet cubicle for whatever was happening there to be inaudible as well as invisible. Linnie would take care of Nita; it was up to Jill to take care of Miss Potgieter. She needed an excuse for being out of bed, but she didn't dare mention the toilet. 'I thought I heard a noise, Miss Potgieter.'

'A noise? Who was making it? Who else was fooling around after lights out? What have I told you girls? Come on now, own up.'

Jill hung her head, trapped between fear of revealing her friends and fear of Potty's fat arms wobbling as they raised the slipper above her head. Everyone feared Potty. She was merciless when it came to beating. She would almost quiver with delight as she surveyed her victim cowering before her, deliberately prolonging the moment to extort maximum pleasure. Jill had been witness and recipient of her assaults more often than she cared to remember, the whistle as the slipper descended, the thwack onto bare bottom-flesh, the searing pain, the burning weals afterwards. She shrank internally at the prospect, casting around wildly for a better story. She could come up with nothing, and Potty was getting impatient. 'You don't know who you were with? Maybe I can jog your memory.' Jill knew what it meant, and held her breath. 'Go and get Maria Morphopolous's slipper.'

Miss Potgieter stood at the top of the stairs, watching her descend to the cloakrooms. Unlike the last time she had gone downstairs at night, the harsh electric light bounced off the concrete and she almost skittered to the bottom. The forty or so girls who used the senior cloakroom all stored their slippers in the foot lockers: rubber flip flops for the most part, bought in the Indian dukas at home, cheap and light and bearable to the skin. But Maria Morphopolous had a different kind of slipper, made of moulded plastic, hard, with ridges in the sole which left a pattern of cuts on the culprit's flesh which lasted for days. Maria Morphopolous's slipper was Potty's most dreaded punishment, reserved for special occasions. This, apparently, was one. Jill found the slipper easily – everyone knew where it was kept – and crept back upstairs to surrender it to the waiting Miss Potgieter. Silently, she followed her back to the door of the dormitory. It wasn't Potty's way to keep her pleasures to herself. She liked to have an audience, even if it was supposedly asleep. She would give Jill's dorm mates the thrill of lying safely in bed and listening to the miscreant being punished. Bend over. Pull down your pyjamas. Tremble of flesh on fat arms. Whistle. Thwack. The gulp and tears that could not be held back. Mummy Mummy Mummy. I want to go home, want to go, want…

It was only after she had stumbled blindly into the dormitory and crawled under the net, after she had sobbed loudly for several minutes, then quietly for several more, after she had shifted and turned to find a place to lie on that didn't hurt, that Jill remembered the others. Just as she was about to sit up and look around her, a hand slipped under the net, followed by a body, then another body. The three of them sat on the bed, their faces a few inches apart, and breathed the few words they dared allow themselves. 'Well done, Jill. You saved us.' Linnie's voice was grave, but Nita's couldn't hide the triumph. 'I did it Jill, thanks to you, I did it. We've fulfilled the Pact – I did the dare, and you didn't tell.' The pain, the outrage, the humiliation melted away. They were the Silent Three, and together they had beaten Miss Potgieter, the rules, and even Maria Morphopolous's slipper.

THE ROAD

I lived at the end of the most notorious road in the country. It took the form of a narrow bush-lined corridor, with space only for two single lanes, which taxi drivers from either end used as a race track to beat their previous best record. The cars they drove were held together by willpower and crammed with people praying for their own survival. They were affectionately known as flying coffins. Lorry drivers hogged the middle of the road, obscuring the view of any oncoming traffic, so all over-taking was done blind at breakneck speed. The god who, because of his affinity for metallic objects, presided over road travel, regularly exacted his dues. The wrecks littering the verges bore testament to his arbitrary vengeance. At night, it was common for lorries to park, unlit, and wait for someone to drive full-tilt into the back of them. A common form of social event in the place where I lived was the thanksgiving service for having escaped a car crash, which alternated with funerals for those who hadn't.

Every time I wanted to leave the small town where I lived and go to the capital, or even just to the university town 80 kilometres away, I had to brave this road. It was a short journey, but familiarity had only increased my dread. I would arrive early at the taxi-park to get the seat behind the driver, having worked out that it was the safest place to be. Next to him was more comfortable, but you went through the windscreen if he had to brake to avoid a head-on collision. The row at the very back was worse, because you had to tilt the middle seat to get in and then you were trapped, and in the event of an accident would probably burn to death while you struggled to free yourself. Although there was no evidence for this, I imagined the driver was also bent on survival and so the best place to be was just behind him in the middle row, and once we started I would sit with my head buried in a book, resolutely not looking at the road. I had come to the conclusion that since I had no control over the car, the driver or the oncoming traffic, I preferred not to see what was coming.

I had been spending a few days in the next town, but there was a four-day holiday coming up and I needed to get back. It was Sallah, the end of the long fast, and everybody else was also going home, so when Kwame offered to drive me I jumped at the offer. Kwame was a student so he could leave when he wanted, and we agreed to set off with plenty of time to spare. The trick was to avoid travelling in that last hour before darkness fell, when the usual recklessness was heightened by the desire to beat the dusk. It was early afternoon when we climbed into Kwame's battered jeep and set out confidently. As though someone in the wings had been awaiting our entrance to flick a switch, the skies opened. The rain was a vertical sheet in front of us, and we were drenched in seconds by water coming in the open sides of the jeep. The park as we passed it was a drift of fog, visibility almost nil, and we hit a go-slow as soon as we joined the traffic. Kwame did an abrupt u-turn and drove back the way we had come, finding the entrance to the house more or less by instinct. We ran heads-down through a wall of water to the shelter of the verandah, where we waited two hours for the rain to slacken. When we set out again, we knew we had lost our safety margin. There was now less than two hours to dusk, and everyone else who was going anywhere had also waited for the rain to stop. The main intersection with its crisscrossing flyovers was a welter of pedestrians, cars and irate policemen. It was Sallah, a four day holiday, and *everyone* had to get home. To add to the usual confusion, the road had become a glutinous soup of thick red mud, which churned and spattered passers-by however carefully you drove. As we sat in the unmoving traffic, a young woman picked her way through the cars ahead of us, nonchalantly retying her spotless pink satin wrapper as she skirted the puddles on delicate toes. Under the flyover, the apparition of a tall skinny man in a long robe loomed at us unexpectedly, a handkerchief tied incongruously around his head. For a moment we were alarmed, then we saw the pile of leather sandals at his feet and recognized him for a Hausa road-hawker sheltering from the rain.

The traffic was tormentingly slow all the way to the junction, but the rain had not driven the hawkers from their livelihood, and we were besieged by the usual offers of biscuits, papers, batteries, cigarettes, calendars, tin-openers, tea towels, knickknacks, paper twists of groundnuts and bottled drinks. Being in an open-sided jeep made us more than usually vulnerable and I was beginning to feel claustrophobic when a siren began its sudden assault on our ears, and an army car pushed its way down the middle of the road, forcing the jeep and other vehicles into the mud of the verges and the crowd. As it passed, a mosquito trail of saloon cars fell into its wake, speeding down the magically created central lane. Kwame let them go before he pulled the jeep back onto the road, carefully avoiding the people standing in his way. As we inched forward, something toppled from a pile of merchandise in a young hawker's arms and rolled into the road. Before she could dart to retrieve it, a passing lorry ground her packet of biscuits into the mud beneath its wheels. A collective sigh rippled along the row of vendors on either side of the road, accompanied by an invocation: 'Ògún, Ògún, Ògún', passing from one to another with a tiny gasp which might have been a strangled laugh. Were they laughing at her misfortune? Or at the antics of the road god, who can snatch an offering from under your nose? He really is a playful fellow, Ògún. He likes to show you wrecks of cars, recently vacated by their occupants in who knows what condition, and the carcasses of dogs he has claimed as a sacrifice. And sometimes, he contents himself with chewing up a packet of biscuits dropped by a small girl. The onlookers appreciated the joke. Mired to the ankles, they were nonetheless energized by the jaunty god's playfulness. On the eve of a Muslim festival, Ògún was reminding us who was in charge.

The traffic thinned at last and Kwame picked up speed. Grumbling, he was comparing the road chaos with Accra where he came from, where he said things were better, much more organized. As we left the hawkers behind, the noise of car-horns and amplified music gave way to the slushing of tyres on the still-wet road. As the bush took over from the town, a slanting ray of late evening sun filtered through the clouds and touched the tops of the palm-trees. The only sign of humanity was the bush-meat seller somewhere along the way, holding up an animal by its tail, like an offering. Kwame brought out some English chocolate, flown in by a friend. It was soft of course, and detaching it from the wrapper occupied us for a few miles. Spirits lifted by our getaway, I quizzed him for the latest gossip and laughed at his stories. Kwame, who had come from a smaller neighbouring country to study, had the unrelenting conviction that all the locals were insane and revelled in presenting the evidence. Two thirds of the way home, I reminded him to stop at the next junction where fruit-farmers from the surrounding countryside displayed their produce at prices much lower than in my local market. As we drew up, Kwame checked his watch. 'Don't be long or we won't make it before dark,' he warned, and sat back to light a cigarette.

Fruit-sellers surrounded the jeep, competing for attention, thrusting examples of their wares through the open sides for inspection. Without hesitation, I allowed one of the women to capture me and carry me off to her stall. There were about half a dozen stalls set back from the road, made of bamboo poles roughly lashed together, and displaying mounds of oranges, grapefruit, pineapples, corncobs in their white wrappers, hands of plantain and bananas and piles of knobbly yams at their feet. It took time to choose, selecting the oranges one by one, inspecting the pineapples for ripeness, negotiating over prices. The fruit-seller placed the oranges in a basket as I picked them, until it was full. She hoisted the basket onto her head and followed me back towards the jeep. Kwame had parked at an angle slightly off the road and as I came around the side of the jeep I stumbled, and was suddenly, horrifyingly, up to my waist in a rudimentary storm drain, full of brackish, moving water. The surface had been so still in the grey light I hadn't taken it for water, and as I broke the surface it fractured into oily black waves which lapped against the edges of the drain. My feet were firmly held by mud but I was immobilised as much by shock as by my invisible anklehold. I heard laughter rise, high as a gong, into the metallic sky. Startled as I was by the fall, I was even more appalled at the way all eyes instantly turned to me, at finding myself suddenly the carrier of the cosmic joke. Being white was bad enough, and I worked hard at making myself inconspicuous, at not minding the calls of 'Òyìnbó!' which greeted all white people everywhere they went. With a slip of the foot my carefully constructed anonymity was blown, and the universal laugh was at my expense. I tried to reach for the side of the ditch and staggered, splashing dirty water on my face where it mingled with tears of humiliation.

A second later, a hand touched mine and I felt myself being hauled out of the shallow drain, black to the waist in mud. People were all around me, forming a protective screen while a man with a bucket of water sluiced my legs. An elderly woman hurried up with a dry wrapper and tied it around my waist. They were smiling, but the laughter had died away as suddenly as it had burst out. Just as it seemed chaos had been about to overwhelm me, order had been restored and I was carried along on the ebbing wave of laughter. I was almost inside the joke myself by now, no longer its object. As the crowd pressed around me I felt the pressure of its expectation.

I was a plaything of Ògún, and while it gave me licence, I had to rise to the occasion. It was a command performance. Smiling, I staked everything on a desperate one-liner, all the speech I could muster at that moment. 'Ògún feràn mi-o, àbí?' I asked. 'Ògún loves me, huh?' Right on cue, the laughter bubbled up again, irrepressible, accompanied by an incredulous, 'Ó gbó Yorùbá. Òyìnbó!' The white woman speaks Yoruba! So, the white clown is human after all.

I judged the moment of my exit, aware that all eyes were still on me as I retreated to the jeep and clambered aboard. The oranges were safely in the back seat, and someone had added a fist of bananas for good measure. Kwame had paid the fruit-seller, who still hovered solicitously. As we drove off, the women were surrounding another car, clamouring again for attention, already oblivious to our departure. The entertainment was over. We reached our destination as the last of the light was fading, the road a strip of darkness leading into the dark. Low on the horizon a thin sliver of moon was just discernible. Sallah had begun.

MASQUERADE

A visit to Lagos is always a welcome contrast to life in the village. Modern anthropology is very demanding, with its insistence on participant observation, being a part of a community, living its life which means forgetting your own. Sometimes the researcher needs to get away, for the sake of remembering who on earth she really is. At least, this researcher does. That's me, Rita Lugard, and before you ask, yes, I am the great-granddaughter of that Lugard, the first Governor of a unified Nigeria, and yes, it was my great-grandmother who named the country after the river Niger. But I am a post-Imperial child and my story is my own. At the time I'm describing, I was living in a small town in Yorubaland in the southwest of the country, doing research on the relationship between oral tradition and contemporary Yoruba language theatre. It was a whole separate world, totally absorbing but also very demanding. I literally ate, thought and slept theatre. It was so intense that every so often I had to escape, and I would make the trip to the city to remind myself there was another world.

On this occasion, I had arrived later than I intended at Ojóta motor park on the outskirts of Lagos. It had taken longer than usual for the taxi to fill up at the start of the journey, and it was already after two by the time we set off. So it was getting towards dusk by the time I caught the bus for Lagos proper, the island which the real Lagosians call by its old name of Èkó. It was a Saturday, and one of the Environmental Sanitation days when, by military decree, you either stayed home or came out and swept the streets, and the city was unnaturally quiet and clean. The big battered yellow transport bus, which normally creaks and groans as it lumbers its way between stops, was able to get up speed, and we actually soared over Third Mainland Bridge and swooped down into Idumota, on the furthest edge of Èkó island. As I stood up to get off the bus, there was a commotion at the door, but I couldn't see because my view was blocked by people. Hats and head-ties were being hastily removed, and so, I realised as I stepped down, were shoes. The people ahead of me were barefoot and bareheaded and talking excitedly, and I caught the word Èyò a split second before I saw them. Masquerades. Suddenly, we were surrounded by at least a dozen veiled and hatted figures, covered from head to foot so that not an inch of skin was exposed, wielding long sticks and dancing to a drum that one of them was carrying. Èyò are the ancestral masquerades of Lagos, and the Èyò festival, I realised, must have been on in spite of Environmental Sanitation. Even the army can't legislate for ancestral spirits, which are ruled by a ritual far older than any modern dictatorship, and as a matter of fact, far more feared and respected. Soldiers can beat you or take your money, lock you up and even kill you, but their jurisdiction ends here, in the world of the living. Ancestral spirits are a visitation from the realm of the departed, whence we came and to which we must all return. Disrespect is an abomination, and no-one wants to pay the price in the spirit world. The way you show respect is by removing your shoes and headgear, and standing still as they dance around you, until they move on of their own accord. Normally, I am ready to do what everybody else is doing, but it was getting dark, and I still had to find my way to Victoria Island to meet up with Steve who was taking me to his Embassy party. This meant I had to have time to wash off the dust, do something with my hair and find something to wear that wouldn't shout from the rooftops that I was living in a village with no mains water and intermittent electricity. I had to look respectable, in other words, and this required some time. So I edged my way little by little along the side of the bus until I was able to disappear round the back of it. It was starting to drizzle, and I had not removed my shoes. My feet were filthy anyway, and I didn't want to add mud to my problems. By some incredible stroke of luck, a taxi was drawing up as I emerged, and I pulled open the door and leapt in. As we moved off, I looked back. It was that time of day when the last dregs of light have almost drained away and everything becomes indeterminate, outlines blur, and you have to squint to be sure of what you're seeing. Besides, a light rain was falling, and the window glass was speckled with drops of dirty water. I can't be sure of what I saw, but I had the strong impression that one veiled figure had separated itself from the rest and was standing quite still at the very spot where I had jumped into the taxi, looking after the retreating car. I shrugged and sat back on the torn seat, preoccupied with reaching Steve's place in time to effect my own transformation.

Embassy parties are not really my cup of tea, but they have the advantage of duty-free delicacies unobtainable elsewhere, and the chance to drink real French wine. I love pepper stew and pounded yam and palm-wine, but sometimes after a few months I hallucinate about cheese and chocolate and coffee and all those city luxuries the expatriates take for granted, and I go to their parties to get a share of the goodies for free. Well, not actually for free, they come at quite a price, as I was beginning to realise as I stood sipping my chardonnay and listening to the man who was talking at me. He worked for one of the big foreign construction companies, and had that conspiratorial air many expatriates adopt when they think they are among their own kind. An Embassy party is actually a tribal gathering, where the white people get together to affirm their identity in a vast ocean of black. If you're there, it goes without saying, you must be one of them.

'So how do you like Nigeria?' was his opening gambit.

'It's hard work, but I love it.' This, I am aware, is not a personal exchange, it is a ritual enactment. Sure enough, the gestural response is all he needs.

'I know exactly what you mean. Mavis and I have been here two years now and we've really tried. It seems Nigerians just have no interest in you if you're not Nigerian. We've invited them home, I play golf with one of the fellows from the company. But you can't – you know – TALK to them, can you?'

I am staring politely, but in my mind I hear the members of the theatre group telling stories as we lie on our backs in the dark after a performance. Talk is their natural medium, extemporising, improvising like jazz musicians, only their medium is words.

'Do you speak any Nigerian languages?' I ask. The man's face is broad and red and registers nothing.

'Why bother? In my job, I don't need to. The managers all speak English, and they're the ones I have to communicate with. It's not English English, if you get my meaning, but you can make them understand. The educated ones anyway, and Mavis speaks pidgin with the houseboy. It's easy. "Me want you put plates in cupboard." It's like a child's language. But then, they are children really, aren't they? At least, that's how I think of them. They don't think the same way we do. I could tell you some horror stories about Nigerians and machinery…'

Over his shoulder, I see the lights twinkling on the lagoon, a canoe glides by in the darkness with the silhouette of a fisherman at its prow. The silence and the dark call to me with the urgent allure of a rescue party to a lost Himalayan climber. I have paid my dues to polite society, I have eaten its cheese and drunk its wine, but I am a fake, and now I want to leave. As I pace the room looking for Steve, I am arrested in mid prowl by a completely unexpected spectacle. It is as if a part of my other life had slipped its mooring and sailed into full view at a Yacht

Club regatta. In a circle of people drinking and talking, silent and motionless, stands a masquerade. Its wide-brimmed hat shadows its face, which in any case is covered in a hood with slits for eyes. Its hands are covered so it appears to have no fingers, and one of them rests on the shaft of a long slim wooden staff. My first reaction is one of embarrassment, as though I am personally responsible for this breach of social etiquette. I glance furtively around, trying to assess the effect of the supernatural gatecrasher on the other guests. I am used to the unexpected, but masquerades are sacred, and they do not belong at Embassy parties. They can also be dangerous, if not treated properly, and I notice the woman next to it is almost burning its arm with her cigarette. Utterly nonplussed, it strikes me then that nobody else has noticed its presence, which means, I suddenly understand, that its business must be with me.

Instinctively, I turn to run. The red-faced man has noticed nothing, he barely registers my departure. I push my way through the throng of people, and am on the street and hyperventilating. Seeing me, the security guard hails a taxi and opens the back door for me. Blindly, I stumble into it, gasping: "Driver, I beg, mek we dey go quick quick. I don late since…"

It's only a few streets to Steve's place, and as we pull up, I lean forward with my taxi fare. The driver half turns and holds out his hand, his face in shadow. With something like an electric shock I notice he has no fingers, or rather, his extended hand is shrouded in cloth, wound tightly around so not an inch of skin is visible. I am half in, half out of the taxi when something tells me to bend down and take off my shoes. I step from the car barefoot, shoes in my hand, avoiding a large muddy puddle in the road. I hear a sound behind me, and turn to look, but nothing's there. The street lies enfolded in darkness like a spent lover, but the only human presence is the Hausa nightwatch at the gate of Steve's apartment building, coming now to undo the padlock.

'Sanu Yusufu,' I mumble gratefully through iron bars. 'Did you see anyone here just now?'

'No madam, na me only,' he responds. 'Master never come. Why you no wear your shoe for road?' he enquires delicately, looking at my feet.

Looking down, I realise my shoes are still in my hand. It was, after all, all that was required. 'For respect,' I say, stepping across the threshold into the safe enclosure of the silent compound.

'LADY'

Let's hope they aren't shooting tonight. Or anyway, let's hope they miss. The car is a capsule, hurtling through darkness. Flyovers stitch and weave above the black hole of the lagoon. Turn up the tape. Robbery, police harassment, random shootings, the state of the roads: recklessness. They think I carry some special protection, 'Omo Oshó Òyìnbó'. Child of the white wizard.

The car heads for the Shrine. I park in a side-alley, and pick my way past the suya stalls redolent with grilling meat, the stalls selling bottled palm-wine or cold fizzy drinks, and make for the stall nearest the door. A crumpled note tossed on the table pays for a handful of spliffs along with the entry fee, and I shoulder my way into the club. The place is still half-empty, but a tension in the air speaks of countdown to Chief Priest's arrival. The band is playing an energetic intro to one of the old songs, the music already too loud for talk, the air thick with smoke. I lower myself onto a battered of tin chair towards the front, sit back and light a spliff.

I've come alone on purpose. There's always a crowd, and tonight I feel like being part of it, the band of followers who regularly congregate here. They come only partly for the music, which has made his name overseas. They come as much to hear Chief Priest speak openly about the things they only mutter over bottles of beer, their discontent pooling on unwiped tables. I guess Chief Priest's charisma has only been made more compelling by his recent bout of detention on charges of possible sedition. I was one of the few journalists who was actually allowed to interview him in jail. It was rumoured that the authorities, confronted by a tall, rangy, slightly dishevelled Englishman, thought I was mad and therefore harmless, and let me in. The only others who made it inside were a couple of columnists on a local news weekly whose editor regularly drinks with senior state security officers. The three of us travelled to the mid-western city where Priest was being held, and visited him together. Apart from the usual political rhetoric which I'm accustomed to hearing, Priest used the occasion to divulge that he had found the secret of eternal youth. He was now getting younger all the time and nothing the military regime could do could stop the process. He was invincible, and when he came out he was going to perform a miracle at the Shrine to demonstrate his possession of supernatural powers. If there's a story in it, I'm there. Don't want to miss the miracle.

But I have another reason for wanting to be here. Six weeks ago, as I was leaving the jail after the interview with Priest, I noticed a young girl standing in the corridor holding a tin plate of food, small and slight, her breasts just points beneath her blouse, her hair natural, her clothes nondescript. It was her eyes that arrested me, large, wide and fearless, returning my look without blinking. I'm used to smart women who look me up and down, taking in the two-day stubble, open shirt, worn jeans and rugged sandals, kissing their teeth and ignoring me. Or, noticing the recording equipment spilling from the pockets of my worn leather shoulder bag, become curious to know more. Or, if I'm lucky, there might be a flush of self-consciousness before their eyes drop, and I know I can offer them a drink or a lift.

This girl did none of these things, was neither superior nor curious nor impressed. Young as she was, she held herself with a striking dignity, taking on all comers with the same even stare. Intrigued, I wondered what she was doing there, alone in a place where grown men feared to go. When I asked who she was looking for, her voice was low but clear and confident. 'Na Chief Priest I for see. Every day I dey bring him chop. He no fit eat this prison food.'

The warder beckoned her towards the cell, where she deposited the plate and came out again. She walked with me and the two columnists out into the prison compound, where she accepted an invitation to go for a drink. We found a shack nearby and ordered beer. She asked for a Fanta and drank it thirstily, like a child. The two guys were joking and teasing her, asking her where she was from and why she wasn't home with her husband. She was from a village further east, she told them, but when she heard Chief Priest was in prison close by, she'd left home, skipped school, and come to town to see what she could do. She had convinced the warders she was a relation, sent to bring food, which she cooked at her auntie's house a few streets away. It didn't add up. If she was a schoolgirl and she'd run away, her aunt would have sent her home. How old was she? Fifteen or sixteen? Chief Priest was a man in his forties, known to have a retinue of women, a prisoner of the state. To most women, he was dangerous, bad and possibly mad.

'You no fear am?' I asked her. 'Chief Priest get powerful jùjú. You no fear wetin he for do you?' She gave me again that appraising look, before she suddenly laughed, a high, delighted laugh. 'He no fit do me anyting,' she responded. 'Chief Priest na my friend. He promise to marry me when he commot for jail, take me go Èkó. I go leave this place soon-soon.' I was taken aback, and it was one of the others who asked her why she wanted to marry an old man. Now for the first time she dropped her eyes. 'Chief Priest no be old,' she said, barely above a whisper. 'He get powerful jùjú for true, wey make him strong and young. Na so-so husband I want, not one old rich man for village.'

Squinting through a cloud of smoke, I remember her words as I sit on the tin chair, waiting for Chief Priest's entry. It's true the man's powerful, but it's the power of words, of saying the things no-one else has the courage to say. Calling some of the country's best-known millionaire businessmen 'international tief-tief'. Calling soldiers zombies. Describing the ruling elite as 'beasts of no nation'. In a climate of fear and intimidation, it translates into a daring that you might call recklessness. The fact that it's irresistible to women accounts for his reputation for sleeping with five or six women a day. I figured out long since that this is part of the superhuman myth the man has successfully woven around himself. So why has this woman bought it? At the prison that day, alone and small but fearless, she struck me as having more to her than that. So maybe she's just a simple village schoolgirl after all.

It's after midnight. We've waited over an hour and I'm starting to get restless, when I become aware of an increase in tension. A sudden commotion at the back of this bamboo shack that calls itself the Shrine; heads turn as a posse of young men stamp down the aisle, and what begins as a murmur builds to a roar. Bàbá-o! Bàbá-o! The man himself, arms raised in a double clenched fist salute, his lithe thin body encased in a skintight electric pink jumpsuit unzipped to the waist, sweeps to the front on a wave of sound. Chief Priest has arrived. He storms the stage in a frenzy of shouting and stamping from his massed acolytes on the floor. The ritual begins.

Smoke hangs in the air, the drums build and build towards a crescendo. Chief Priest begins to talk to the crowd, about jail, about what they tried to do to him. 'They say I smoke Indian hemp, but I tell them, the only hemp wey I ever smoke grow right here for Nigeria.' The trademark tantalising of the audience: 'This song call B.O.N.N.' The laugh, before he decodes: 'Beasts of No Nation'. Then he starts to sing, and at the words 'Animal can't dash me human rights', the whole place erupts. Everybody's standing, dancing, woven together by the music and the magnetism of the man on stage. Then the women

73

come out to join him, the movement of their bodies an emanation of the music, waists gyrating, backs to the crowd, stripteasing with clothes on. The mounting sexual excitement is palpable, embodied in Chief Priest himself, who struts and parades in front of the dancers. Their sexuality may be on display but it indisputably belongs to him. Madness and mastery. Whatever you think of him, the man knows how to create a spectacle – like the day he married his entire dance troupe of twenty-seven women in one ceremony because people were calling them prostitutes.

He leaves the stage for a few minutes and the dancers take over. My eyes come to rest on one of them. Completely absorbed in the music, her face is rapt, her eyes almost closed as her body performs its sinuous winding movements. The small breasts are barely covered by a thin strip of cloth, her midriff bare and daubed with paint, her face heavily made-up with glitter highlighting the eyes and cheekbones. But I know it's her, the girl from the jail, and a heat comes over me as I watch her. At that moment, Chief Priest returns to the stage, naked to the waist, his face, chest and back daubed with white, and leads the women in a call and response, their high reedy insistent voices counterpoising his deeper solo. In the confusion of feelings – anger, desire, pity – anger predominates. How can she be content to be one of Priest's women? To put herself on display, to sell herself so cheap, for what? The spurious glamour of being in his orbit, the chance to hang around him in case he decides to bestow the favour of requiring her services? Through the anger, I'm conscious of another feeling – disappointment. I leave my seat and head for the toilets at the back, pushing past a drunk who's swaying across my path, stepping over the pool of urine that's starting to seep across the raw concrete floor. The stink is so bad I gag, and make for the door, stepping with relief into the tepid night air of the street.

Outside, I light a cigarette and lean against the flimsy

bamboo wall of the shack. With the smoke, I inhale the scent of frying àkàrà and the rancid smell of stagnant drains. It's three in the morning, and the street is alive with raucous conversation, people coming and going, cars revving, the cries of hawkers offering cigarettes, chewing gum, kola nuts, matches, aspirin. Against my back, the wooden structure vibrates to the music, led by Chief Priest's voice intoning: 'Human rights na my property. Animal can't dash me human rights.' Surrendering to the insistence of the long-drawn out climax, I close my eyes, feeling each shudder and tremor on my skin, my breathing following the rhythm of the song. Someone is breathing next to me, just out of synch. I can feel the warmth of her body against my arm, and when I open my eyes, she's looking straight into them, with that frank and disconcerting gaze. The exaggerated make-up is gone, and with it the look of a chief's concubine. She is herself only, and when I ask how she is, she responds gaily, without inhibition. 'I wan come cook rice for you. You get meat for house?'

In the months that follow, Ngozi becomes a fixture in the large, half-empty apartment, coming and going at will and without warning. She arrives early in the morning, dressed for the street in a new print wrapper and head-tie, her skin glowing, her movements full of energy as she changes into the old wrapper she keeps in my cupboard. She's happy, it seems, just to inhabit this space, making no demands and showing no expectations. While I read papers or bang out a story, she sweeps the house, washes my clothes, fills the buckets with water, even though I keep telling her I don't want a household slave. She laughs as if forgiving a foreigner's breach of etiquette. Sometimes she asks for money and disappears for an hour or so, returning with bunches of fresh green leaves and dried fish, tins of tomato paste and hot peppers, onions and chunks of meat bought from the Hausa butcher. Then she performs a mysterious alchemy in the kitchen, the aroma gradually becoming so distracting I can no longer think about anything else. When I hear the thud thud thud of the pestle in the mortar, I surrender and go and watch her pounding yam, throwing the heavy pestle in the air, bringing it down with a thump that jars her body, sweat glistening on her forehead which she wipes off on the sleeve of her wrapper without missing a beat. Until she came, I had never noticed the pestle and mortar pushed against a wall. I usually buy food ready cooked from one of the sellers a few streets away, or eat in a restaurant, or get by on bread and coffee. Waiting for water to boil is all I have the patience for and the only cooking skill I possess. In contrast, her meticulous cleaning and scraping, peeling and frying and simmering, the acrid smell of hot palm oil softening into something sweet and enticing as she adds ingredients one by one, strike me as possessing the attributes of art. The rendering of yams, hard and knobbled as prehistoric roots, into the fragrant, steaming mound of pure white she puts on the table is nothing short of miraculous. Next to it, the soup shimmers under a layer of shining palm oil, tomato-red alternating with leaf-green in the depths of the rough clay bowl she brought home one day from the market. I don't generally notice hunger, but when she cooks, I eat like a refugee. It's only now I understand that what she offered was not subservience. Instead, I realize, it was a gift, a votive offering in a ritual of which she was celebrant and priestess.

Only rarely will she stay all night, generally making her quiet exit sometime after dark. It's hard to get her to talk about herself, but one stifling mosquito-ridden night, one of the few times she sleeps in the apartment, both of us lying on my narrow, iron-sprung bed, she tells me what I need to know. She was proud to be one of the older girls at the school the politicians had built in her village. At fifteen, she was working towards the WAEC exams, had her eye on a typing course and maybe a job in an office in town, when her father announced she was to be married. When she found out the bridegroom was an old friend of her father's, someone she had known all

76

her life, whose three wives she knew, whose children were her schoolmates, she cried and begged to be allowed to finish school. Her imaginings of her own future had not included being the fourth wife of an old man and staying in the village for the rest of her life. She had seen the pictures on her father's television and knew there was more to the world than that. Elsewhere in the same country, women dressed up and drove cars to work, chose who to marry and how many children they would have. She wanted to be one of those women, not poor and ignorant and overworked like her mother. Waiting on her father and his friends one evening, she had seen pictures of a man they called Chief Priest standing outside a courtroom, his clenched fist raised, and heard a voice explaining that he was a danger to society, a currency smuggler and hemp smoker, and that he was in jail, but that he had been there nearly two years and was soon coming out. Her attention had been caught because, unlike most of the pictures, this was of someone she knew. She and her friends listened to his music on the radio, and some of them had cassettes which they danced to, singing along to the words: 'Call a woman African woman/ She go say I be lady-o/She go say I no be woman… She go say she equal to man/She go say she get power like man/She go say anything man do/She sef fit do…' They had to be careful, because their parents didn't approve of the songs, which heightened the pleasure and lent the music an aura of rebellion and danger. She was leaving the room when she caught the name of the prison they were keeping him in: it wasn't in Èkó, where he lived, it was in another city, in their part of the country, a city she had been to once on the bus with her mother when they went to visit her aunt who had married a man who lived there.

When it became apparent that her pleas and tears were not going to make any difference, that her father's decision was made and nothing would change it, Ngozi came to a decision of her own. She was going to the city where Chief Priest was in prison, she was going to find him and beg him to take her with him back to Èkó. The voice on the television had said he would be out of jail soon. She had heard he liked women and had many wives, but treated them well and allowed them to dance on stage in his nightclub and show their bodies and smoke cigarettes. She wanted to be a woman like that, not a farmer with a baby on her back. So she left and went to the city, walking miles out of the village to a place where she knew the bus stopped on the road and she could get on it without being seen. She had found her way to her aunt's house with difficulty, but once there, she had told her aunt her parents had sent her because they could no longer afford her school-fees, and could her aunt please find her something to do. It was not unusual for children to be sent to stay with family in the town, and her aunt accepted the story, especially since she herself had a business to run and had just had her third child, so she welcomed Ngozi as a godsend.

'Didn't she notice you cooking food and carrying it out of the house?' I ask. 'Me sef, I start to sell small small things for street,' she replies, 'cigarette and kola and salt and soap powder, and the money wey I make I keep. Na so I go buy meat and rice for Chief Priest.' 'But what did your aunt think about you going to the jail? About you visiting a convicted criminal?' 'Criminal?' She looks at me wonderingly, as if my ignorance were so profound she can only pity me. 'Chief Priest no be criminal. Everybody sabi na military government wey put innocent man for prison. My aunt na city woman, she too know all about soldier. No be soldier wey dey come for market, overturn her stall, burn her wares, kill people? She tell me say, go my daughter, Chief Priest go know this town get good people as well as Èkó.'

I'm impressed by her clarity and lack of ambivalence. I know, as well as she does, that soldiers rough up women, that beatings and rapes are common, that she was taking a risk in publicly associating with Chief Priest. But something still niggles at me, and drives me to pursue her further. 'And so, now you're in Èkó, in Chief Priest's compound, isn't it just like being an old man's wife?' I ask. 'Only instead of being four, there are dozens of you. How often do you get to see him? Don't the women fight over him?' Ngozi sighs and closes her eyes. I understand the conversation is over, but the dissatisfaction remains. I need to see for myself what it is that keeps Ngozi in thrall to the man, even while she cooks for *me* and sleeps with *me*.

There are competing views of why she's here. According to a woman journalist who visits off and on, the girl's no better than a prostitute. She and Ngozi are from the same part of the country, and she's adamant that she can have only one motive for hanging around a white man. 'She wants money, of course. You wait, you'll see. Either she'll ask for it or she'll take it. There'll be a sick relative, or some such excuse, and once she's got what she wants, she'll take off, and you won't see her again.' Another woman friend is less brutal, but tends to agree. 'What else can she be after? It's not sex; she's with Chief Priest. What he doesn't have is money, and you're a white man. She can't see you any other way.' But worse than their scepticism is the open admiration of one of the foreign correspondents. As far as he's concerned, she's the ultimate in exotica, a dancer at the Shrine, touched with Chief Priest's aura of sexual excess and male power. He wants to know how she performs in bed, for God's sake, and he won't leave it alone. 'Is it true black women are hot? Does she let you lick her? I hear black men refuse to lick. How about her, does she do it to you?' He only sleeps with white women – 'I don't want to catch anything, man' – but he regards all women in basically the same way. I hate the way men like that assume some kind of camaraderie, but I work with the guy and I don't know how to deflect it without creating an incident. It's the price of being white in a black country, other ex-pats assume you're the same as them. Then one day, Fabian arrives. He turns up at the apartment on one of his impromptu visits to the city, to remind me of my promise to introduce him to Chief Priest. Fabian's a musicologist, living in a village to the north and studying the influence of tradition on contemporary musical forms. Funds are low and I spot a radio item in it. If I'm honest, it's the chance I've been looking for.

It's nothing unusual for foreigners to visit The Republic. Chief's compound is an island of sound and movement in the quiet residential backwater, pulsating Afrobeat vying with the shouts of women, children screaming, the slamming of car doors as messengers are dispatched on errands. The arrival of a battered yellow taxi, and the emergence of two white men hung around with cameras and recording equipment, hardly attracts attention. The guard at the gate recognizes me from previous visits, and gestures for us to come inside. We're shown into a shabby waiting room, where we sit in a couple of well-worn cushion chairs until we're called. A naked child wanders through, pursued by a young girl who might be his mother. Like all Priest's women, she's fearless and unimpressed by our presence, dropping a cursory curtsey but hardly glancing at us. The only decoration in the room is a giant poster of Priest giving his customary clenched fist salute, with the words 'Black President' splashed in red across his lower half. Fabian leans forward restlessly. 'What do you think he's doing?' he mutters. 'Is this just for show?' I laugh. 'What would you be doing if you had twenty-seven wives and assorted concubines? It's a full-time job keeping them all satisfied.' Fabian looks impressed, but disbelieving. 'When does he get time to make music?' he asks. 'Why don't you ask him?' I suggest. 'He's bound to have an answer. He's got one for everything.'

Forty minutes pass in desultory conversation beneath the larger-than-life image on the wall, before one of the ubiquitous hangers-on calls us inside. Chief Priest is ensconced in his personal sanctum in an immense armchair. Apart from a couple of smaller chairs, the only other furniture is an enormous music system with standing speakers six feet high against the end wall. The walls reverberate to the beat of one of his own instrumental arrangements, loud enough to drown out any human voice. He greets us without getting up by means of a clenched fist half raised towards us. He's wearing nothing but a pair of shocking pink underpants and his head is wreathed in smoke from a fat spliff, which he passes to me as soon as we sit down. I obediently take a drag and offer it to Fabian, who hesitates for a second. I catch his eye and Fabian gives way with a good grace. I know the score; you don't set the pace of these interviews, you leave that to Priest himself. You can try to hurry him along, mindful of your broadcasting deadline or the curfew or just something else you have to do, but all that achieves is further withdrawal on his side, a deepening of his ironic detachment. Once you enter the Republic, time itself comes under the sway of its President. It's better to inhale deeply and adjust your rhythm. He might make you wait, but he's not going to disappoint you.

Seven hours later, dishevelled and red-eyed, we stand again in the road outside the compound, while one of Priest's boys goes for a car. It's a dark night, but we're in Priest's territory and there's nothing to fear. Our hearing adjusted long ago to the blast of sound, which Priest obligingly lowered during the recording. We exchange a wordless look, and slap palms in gleeful triumph. We're high and not just on smoke. 'Man,' says Fabian softly, 'what a guy. Now I know what makes him think so much of himself. He really is a phenomenon.' Already acquainted with Priest's powers of seduction, I'm less ready to be impressed, but even I feel elated. I knew Priest was a consummate performer, projecting the image of a man of the people, one with the working poor, mouthpiece of the voiceless, cock of the walk, symbol of sexual potency to encourage the impotent, tormentor of authority, exposer of hypocrisy, ruthless critic of corruption, satirist of the foibles of the powerful. But there's another side to him, one that he doesn't parade in public, that he showed us this afternoon and evening.

Despite the smoke and the underpants, the man we sat and talked with had been the western-educated, aristocratic son of an elite family, christianised and literate for generations, politically astute, articulate, soft-spoken and courteous. Trained in music at an overseas academy he talked knowledgeably about the technicalities and intricacies of his own and others' musical forms, tradition and innovation, influence and interaction. We found he could talk about anything, from western classical conventions to the language of the talking drum, from jazz to blues to township jive, apala to hiphop, juju or reggae. He had Fabian mesmerised by his charismatic connectivity between worlds, a shapeshifter juggling with words and images. I sat and twiddled the dials on the Sony, forgetting to worry about the broadcast. Editing for highlights was going to be like trying to separate out a single strand of a kaleidoscope.

In the course of the evening, Priest calls for drinks, and the floor begins to fill with empty bottles of Star. After a few hours, three women come and kneel before Priest, and then proceed to bring in stools and bowls of water for washing, before serving each of us an earthen bowl of egusi soup accompanied by pounded yam. We eat and talk, the women take the bowls away and bring water for our hands again. As I dip my hand in the plastic container, I realise with a shock that I know the hands which hold it, know those polished fingernails and the darker folds of skin over the knuckles, the slim wrist, the smooth skin disappearing into the sleeve of a silken wrapper. My eyes meet hers, and she's smiling, unafraid, as if we were alone in the apartment and she had cooked just for me. She looks not in the least discomforted, whereas my face burns and I lose concentration, letting the tape run without adjustment from then on.

When the moment arrives when Chief Priest is ready to let us go, he finally rises from his chair, a thin, wiry man, shorter than me by several inches. As Fabian packs up his equipment, Priest speaks just loud enough for me to hear and no-one else.

'That one na fine fine sisi, no be so?' he says, conversationally. 'She no be lady-o, my brother. That one na African woman for true.' And he begins to sing softly, lines from his famous song of a decade before: 'African woman go dance she go dance the fire dance/ She know him man na master/She go cook for am/ She go do anything he say....' For a moment only, I glimpse something atavistic – pride, cruelty? – before the urbane, cultured persona takes over and genially says good-bye, do come again. So abrupt and subtle is the transition, that I think I may have imagined it. Once on the street, I'm able to participate in Fabian's excitement at the coup we've pulled off in getting the continent's most controversial musician to reveal his private thoughts about his music. But I remain disturbed, uncertain how to translate to myself the words Priest has spoken. What I do understand is that some sort of a challenge has been issued, which sooner or later will have to be answered.

Ngozi comes several times after that, her behaviour the same mixture of calm practicality and sensuous teasing as always, and for a while, I allow myself to believe that nothing has changed. But I take to delaying tactics when she's leaving, trying to prolong the time she spends with me, to spin it out indefinitely and trick her into staying. I wait till she begins to change out of the old house wrapper and into her street clothes to come up behind her and pulling her against me, tease her nipples in the way I know she can't resist, just as I can't resist the pressure of her taut buttocks against my crutch. But she pulls away, laughing, insisting she has to go, and extricates herself, tying her wrapper with one hand as she fends me off with the other. Her nipples are still erect under the flimsy fabric as she backs laughing out of the door, and I'm sore and turgid with desire.

One night, seeing her standing naked before the wardrobe where she has carefully hung her clothes, I can't bear it any longer. Without the soft intimacies that are our usual prelude to lovemaking, I take hold of her from behind, and throw her face down on the bed, falling across her back and forcing her legs apart. There's a hum in my ears, and I hear myself groaning, but Ngozi is silent, lying unmoving till I judder to a sweaty panting halt. When I roll off her, she slides off the bed and calmly proceeds to dress, as though nothing has happened. But she never comes again.

As the weeks turn into months, I work so many hours my friends start to doubt my sanity. I'm possessed by the feeling that I have destroyed something, and guilt hounds me. This feeling pursues me even to the neighbouring country where I go to cover a coup. Surrounded by limbless victims of rebel attacks, under fire, all I can think of is Ngozi, all I can see her face as she leaves my flat for the last time.

Then one day, I'm given another assignment. Chief Priest is to headline a massive outdoor concert at the sports stadium, which is being unofficially billed as a musicians' protest against the continuing presence of the illegal military regime. Officially, it's a fund-raiser for the children of detainees, in itself a provocation, but not enough to have the concert banned. A foreign radio station wants live coverage, so I go, telling myself it's just a job, but undeceived by my own attempt at self-delusion. I've carried the pain of losing her for months, and I know I'm going for Ngozi, in the hope of seeing her and somehow resolving the lurking shame which is her legacy.

I arrive at the stadium in a car with a journalist from one of the city's big weekly journals. Délé, who always wears a shirt and tie, is soft-spoken and smooth and has a way of talking himself into anywhere he wants to go, and out again afterwards. It's a useful characteristic in a place where press passes alone don't always guarantee entrance, particularly if you refuse to bribe. Délé's driving, and as we come across the flyover and pull into the nearside lane to descend to the stadium, we both gasp at what we see beneath us. 'Shit! What have they brought out the armoured vehicles for?' 'They want to make trouble, my brother,' Délé responds softly, slowing the car to a crawl. Police cars are ranged on both sides of the entrance to the stadium, armoured cars parked at a safe distance, waiting. 'For what?' I ask again. 'It's just to scare us,' says Délé, sounding unperturbed. 'They're expecting 30,000 people, so they have to show they're in control. They're afraid if Chief Priest starts talking about cancelled elections, structural adjustment, or any of the other things he likes to talk about, that people may get excited. So they're here as a warning.' 'Not much use against a miracle,' I point out, 'that's what he's promising for tonight after all. They'll need more than armoured vehicles to contain that.'

The concert has been billed to start at two pm. It's nearly seven as we gain the VIP entrance and show our passes, which let us into the performing area. A ragged reggae outfit is jamming limply on stage, and we head to the bar to see who else is there. The stands are half-full, people filtering in slowly, security guards at every turn, swaggering, half-bored. In the guests' bar, beer, greetings, a sense of suppressed expectation. Gradually a chant starts to gather force outside, 'Bàbá-o! Bàbá-o!' and I turn to see Chief Priest make his entrance from the far end of the stadium, dressed in white, surrounded by his bodyguards, similarly dressed in white. They move as a group, literally storming the stadium, Chief Priest running to one side and stopping dead, punching the air in his characteristic salute, the young men at his heels. Then he turns, darting to the other side, stopping dead again, the young men rushing to his side. The ever-growing crowd goes wild, screaming its approval. On stage, a slow warm-up of the instruments is in progress, horns riffing, percussion dimly in the background, the faint tapping of a drum. After the excitement of Chief Priest's entrance, anticlimax. People are standing on the terraces, grouped towards the front, contained by the wire fence. Then a burst of sax, pure and mellifluous, and Chief Priest is suddenly on stage.

As he attacks the keyboard, the first strains of a familiar tune rising like incense into the humid darkness, a rebellion begins amongst those who are penned in on the terraces. Unaware, I've left the bar and I'm wandering towards the stage, to which my press pass gives me access, when I notice security guards running for the fence. People are filtering onto the pitch, escaping from the confines of the meshed-in terraces, more and more of them. The guards are having trouble holding the gates, as bodies build up against them, rocking backwards and forwards. A couple of bodies hurtle across the fence, others begin to scramble up and it sways dangerously. Frozen for a second, my journalist's instinct comes to my rescue, and I sprint for the stage, pulling out the Sony as I run. A line from one of Priest's songs teletexts across my vision: 'If trouble come, yanga go meet am.' Whatever happens, I'm there to record it.

I gain the stage at the very moment when Chief Priest steps forward, gesturing to the instrumentalists to be quiet. From the terraces, missiles are being thrown, bottles are smashing on the track, a woman is cut by flying glass and screams, holding her face. Unable to hold back the crowd, guards are striking out with slabs of wood as people scatter across the pitch. Throwing both arms in the air, Priest shouts into the mike: 'Easy now, my brothers, easy. Make we no fight, I beg. Make everyone come for front, guards too, everyone.' The dun dun player steps to his side and raps out the same message, the old language stilling the activity on the ground. In the momentary pause, Chief Priest continues, lowering his voice to barely a whisper, caressing the mike with his breath, so the air is filled with the sound of his breathing, gradually taking shape as words: 'My friends, we no be animal. If anybody com tell us we be animal, it no be true at all at all. No be our leaders sef wey say, "This uprising will bring out the beast in us"? No be Pik Botha, na him president for South Africa? No be us, we no be animal. Una sabe how for tell who be animal in human skin? He wears suit or agbada as disguise, and he drives Mercedes.' Behind the words, a tune is starting to take shape, and Chief Priest steps back abruptly to merge with the instrumentalists.

Throughout this performance, my eyes have been riveted on Priest, except for a couple of glances at recording levels. Now, as I turn my attention to the grounds I see that a miracle has taken place. The same people who were scuffling and fighting a few minutes previously are dancing with each other, guards and audience both. What had threatened to become another item in a catalogue of violent cliches has spontaneously transformed itself into a playground. Two men have made themselves into a swing, with a third on their clasped hands, swinging to the beat of the music. A tall man in a Fulani hat and dark glasses is flirting with a woman in an immaculate silk wrapper and high heels, dancing ever more suggestively in front of her, and she's laughing. From nowhere, a flotilla of tiny girls has appeared with plastic bags, out of which they sell frozen banana ice lollies. Young men in tattered clothes hold up life-size portraits of Chief Priest for sale; as well as a playground, it's a marketplace. A huge uniformed guard blissfully sucks a lolly, swaying gently as the instruments build their wall of sound and the repetitive phrases circle above it: 'My people are useless, my people are senseless, my people are undisciplined. Which kind talk be that? Government talk be that, animal talk be that.'

Turning back to the stage, I'm once again frozen with shock. A line of women is dancing in the middle of the stage, their exposed skin painted in elaborate designs, faces heavily made up, eyes and lips accentuated, cheeks highlighted, earrings dangling, feet bare, a narrow strip of cloth stretched across breasts, waists swaying. No more than a few feet from me is Ngozi, apparently oblivious to everything but the music and the movements she is sinuously and provocatively performing. Her lithe body is one with the song's rhythm, her face rapt, her eyes half-closed, transported as I have seen her many, so many times, in different circumstances, to a different tune. Music and movement blur together, so that I can no longer distinguish who is singing, or which instrument is playing, and instead all sound is focused in her body, and it is her body which sings, demanding my response. And though I never dance, I start to move, standing in one corner of the huge stage, bag at my feet, Sony round my neck, aware of nothing any longer but the moment and the sensation of dancing, which links me to her, and to the crowd which moves in unison, as though driven by a common energy, a single heart beat. And as the climax approaches, Priest leads us in a spontaneous call and response in which everybody joins. 'Animal can't dash me,' sings Priest and pauses for the thousands of voices to roar back: 'Human rights!'

And again, 'Human rights na my property! So therefore?'

'You can't dash me my property!'

'Animal can't dash me?'

'My property!'

And finally, the authoritative voice of Chief Priest, the high-pitched voices of the dancers, the multiple voices of the crowd, merge together in one prolonged chorus, 'Animal in human skin! Beasts of no nation!' over and over, encircling the stage, the stadium, the slumbering armoured vehicles, the sleeping soldiers, the city with its barracks and prisons, its slums and marketplaces, its lagoons and flyovers, swirling upwards on eddies of air and outwards to the ocean, scattering on the wind.

LOOKING FOR ÒSUN

THE TOWN AND THE SACRED GROVE

Òsogbo is a town like many Yoruba towns. In the harmattan, the wind from the north covers it in dust, obliterating its secrets under a red blanket which melds everything – walls, roofs, roads, dogs, chickens, children – into one undifferentiated whole. It looks dirty, unkempt, forlorn. Galvanised roofs turn to rust, mud walls appear to be reverting to their origins, drying and disintegrating into the choking air, where dust hangs in a red mist, rising from the red road, falling from the parched sky. In the streets, people wrap their faces against the dust, which coats the inside of nostrils and tickles the back of the throat. A dry rasping cough is the town itself gasping for breath.

In the rains, the water which pours unceasingly from a leaden sky beats the galvanise like a drum and pours itself in rivulets into the road, where it mixes with the red earth to become a river of mud. Life is suspended, waiting for the rain to stop. People huddle together on verandahs, dogs slink into doorways, and goats stand motionless under the dripping trees. Cars pass slowly, splashing red mud up the sides of the houses, negotiating potholes which have grown from puddles to lakes. If they fall in, they're stuck till the rains end, tomorrow or next week or in September.

Then one day you come to Òsogbo, and it's transformed itself again. The bush that presses at the margins of the town is brilliant with new growth, and green sprouts where before there was only red dust or mud. The town looks washed, it sparkles with life. The streets bustle; the air vibrates with cries of women offering beancakes for sale, luring customers to their neat piles of pepper and tomatoes spread on banana leaves and cardboard; the high tone of iron striking metal rings insistently from somewhere out of sight. A whistle pierces the noise and on the outskirts of the town a train arrives at the station, goods are unloaded, trucks clog the streets as wares are distributed to the shops. Suddenly, Òsogbo is thriving, pulsing with commerce. All the multifarious goods which underpin existence are on display on the street: bolts of cloth, padlocks, carved calabashes, kola nuts, baskets, bags, mats, gourd rattles hanging from a pole, mounds of yellow garri, heaps of green leafy vegetable, slabs of meat and a beefy man chopping it, two boys playing ping pong across a rough hunk of wood, a child screaming as a man beats him with a stick. A forest of signs bristles around them, enticing you to art shops, printers, barbers, beauty parlours, repair shops, laundries, tailor shops, sewing and typing schools, chop spots with illustrated menus, bars with murals of lip-painted ladies, medicine stores. A jungle of words and images jostles for your attention.

At the heart of all this intense vitality, the Ààfin, seat of the Oba, the king, and across the road, the Oba's market, stand sentinel, shoulder to shoulder. What are they guarding? What secrets do they protect from the eyes of outsiders, what rivalries, what struggles for power? At the centre of the market is its shrine, devoted to the god Alájéré. Born of a lioness, he is the divine principle of childhood, and therefore naked, vulnerable, detached from all material possessions, a wanderer entirely devoted to his mission – 'the transformation of opposing premonitions into life through a mystical process of evolution'. His feet stand on a small hill of laterite inside the shrine, but someone has hacked off his body. Perhaps its nakedness was an offence, perhaps it was too powerful, too undefended. Outside, the mosque confronts the Ààfin, the amplified wail of the muezzin contesting with the hawkers' cries: *All-ah akbar*, five times a day, calling on the faithful to turn to Mecca. Long before jihad brought the new religion down from the north along with the harmattan and the red dust, before missionaries arrived from across the sea, local deities held sway over town, bush and river. The slow brown stretch of water that snakes and coils its way around the town embodies Òsun, the goddess who has guarded Òsogbo through the centuries. Now her rule is disputed, her rituals regarded as pagan, and developers are hungry for her sacred grove.

The car is a typical local taxi, battered and stripped to essentials: inside, the door mechanism is exposed, the road is visible through holes in the floor. The driver, whiplash-lean, guns the accelerator, unable to stop in case the car won't start again, slowing down enough for you to leap in and state your destination: the grove of Òsun. The car swerves off the main road, past the crumbling Brazilian houses with their neatly swept front yards and grandiose elephant sculptures, and suddenly the town has ended and you are in the bush. The road cuts a swathe through the forest which presses in on either side, confining intruders to a narrow ribbon of red dust. You bump on the springless seat as the taxi jolts along, through vegetation so thick and exuberant it appears impenetrable. Organic sculptural shapes bound in the sinewy arms of creepers are alive with a nameless but palpable energy, and it's with a sense of surprise that you realise a human hand has been at work. Forms are emerging from the mud of the verges. Earth but not earth, animal, bird and human, they peer ambivalently at the dust-devouring creature, part metal, part human, which grinds its way further and further into the forest. They guard the margins of the sacred grove, and now the creature disgorges you from its belly, and you are at the gateway.

After noise, silence. Your ears sing with a profound quiet which falls like water all around you, in sibilant whisperings which only deepen the reverential hush. Òsun, the goddess of the waters of life, beckons you forward. You step from the road into a maze of spirals, whorls and curlicues, a corridor which mirrors the meanderings of the river itself. Unimpeded, water takes the shape it chooses: shell, womb, calabash, river, ocean. Without Òsun, creation is impossible. Her symbols – egg, shell, snail, spiral – are the basic matter of life itself, the double helix which repeats itself in every living form. Here in the grove, these symbols proliferate, as if the grove itself were an egg at the centre of a spiral. Statues are everywhere, gods and animals shaped out of the very earth on which they stand. The Yoruba way of worship expresses itself through art, which transforms material forms into spiritual symbols. And here, the clay statues provide a physical refuge for the gods they represent: Orisanla, Alájéré, Iyemoo, Sanponna, Obatala, Òsun… The grove is an oasis where the gods can rest and be at peace, in the embrace of the forest.

At the centre of the spiral sits a shrine, where a babalawo throws cowries to divine your present consciousness and foretell the future. 'You are a child of the goddess, *omo Olókun*. You will always return.' The cowries fold in upon themselves, like the lips of a vulva, promise of fruition. Two palmfuls of water pour from a calabash drawn from the river. Again and again, like ever widening ripples in a pool, from further and further across the water, the goddess leads you to this spot. She stands tall at the river's edge, she holds out her arms. Green with moss, she rises from the earth, her feet one with the river bank. She welcomes you, she invites you to the water where barren women come to bathe and be made fertile. She offers you her gifts. From a clump of slender bamboo, a tiny leaf twirls slowly at the end of a cobweb. A leaf-coloured butterfly opens its wings to brilliant blue and yellow. A brown water-snake slides through the brown water. The river offers its liquid body to fingers of sunshine, to wind which caresses its quivering surface. The river's bass and treble is in your ears – sound of bells, a cowhorn, chanting. Alájéré and Òsun are fire and water. Together they create life, bringing all oppositions into balance. Town and grove are adjacent realities bonded by a stream of sacred water. But the refuge of Alájéré, the wooden statue, is severed and Òsun's grove is hacked and violated. How long can they maintain their timeless tension, how long retreat into the foetal spiral where the vital secret is enwombed? Throw the cowries, ask the question. The answer is elusive as water dropping from a calabash, but the question is open-ended, and the answer always exceeds the question.

2:
CARNIVAL

The turboprop drops from a clear blue sky and bumps to a halt on the runway at Piarco. The speaker system crackles its last message: 'Thank you for choosing LIAT and welcome to Carnival.' Clustered around the terminal entrance, a group of pan-players fills the air with sound. In my eagerness, I've come without the address where I'm staying, and the Immigration officer allows me to write 'Auntie Brenda' on the customs form. Outside, a smiling woman welcomes new arrivants with a rum punch. The calypso belting out of the loudspeakers is interrupted by a commercial: 'Have you got your sunblock, your water, your Durex condom? Because in the heat of the moment, anything can happen. Make sure you have your Durex condom!' It's Carnival in Trinidad, and I am here, in Port of Spain. You inhale excitement just by breathing the air. It's as if a few million people – the entire population – have all caught something at the same time. I am on the edge of my seat in the taxi as it joins the mad swirl towards the city, and from my quickened pulse rate I know I'm catching it too.

In the Church calendar, it's the week before the beginning of Lent. The whole island is partying. Purists complain that old Mas has gone and Carnival has lost its meaning. There's no longer any need for slaves to mock or parody their masters, to roam the streets with unbridled licence. Instead, Carnival has been reduced to an occasion for bodily display and extravagant spending. But next day I am out shopping in the centre of town when a troupe of devils materialises in the crowd. The frame freezes, the busy street metamorphoses into a medieval morality play. Satanic emissaries with long black tails stride down the middle of the road, flicking at well-dressed shoppers with their whips. A devil chained by the ankle climbs a wall, writhing and twisting in the heat of unseen flames, until it's dragged by its chain out of the picture. It's stifling among the close-packed shops with people pressing into them in search of make-up, glitter, tights. But the chill the devil casts as it passes hangs in the air like the whiff of an underground drain.

Scene one, panyard. I'm taken aback when we arrive at a shabby concrete lot carved out of a residential district. It might be a car park, or a building site, or just a space where a derelict building has been knocked down. There's an open area in front of an awning, underneath which are the pans. What did I expect? Twenty pans on a float, like at Notting Hill? Or welcoming tourists at the airport with a touch of the 'authentic' Caribbean? Under the awning is an orchestra of maybe two hundred pans – tenor pans, bass pans, little pans, big pans – two hundred people with one totally rapt expression, all playing their different parts, subsumed in the music. Otherwise, only a rudimentary bar for a shot of rum or bottles of Carib, a brazier for serving corn soup. No chairs, no ceremony, just knots of people standing attentively in front of the players, like fishermen poised at the fringe of the surf. At first, all they hear is its overwhelming roar, but little by little their ears distinguish its orchestral elements, the long sigh as the sea gathers itself and flings itself forward to crash at their feet, the suck and whisper as it pulls at the sand, rattling the pebbles in its slow retreat. After the first impact, I surface enough to notice that, apart from the pans, there's a raised platform at the back on which stands a group of musicians with all sorts of extraordinary instruments. Someone's scraping a sort of circular cheese grater with a thing like a whisk. There are cowbells, shakers, every old bit of iron beaten and rung and clanged and clunked, all led by a guy with a metal gong which looks like a bit from a mechanic's yard, which he beats with a metal stick. It looks like a convention of scrap-iron merchants. It's the engine room: the rhythm section. It exerts an irresistible, tidal pull, so that I find myself winding my way inside the pan-stands till I'm standing right underneath it.

The noise is absolutely incredible. At my back, the incessant sound of struck steel, while all around me the aluminium poles holding up the stands are vibrating, the air's vibrating, my organs are vibrating, my eardrums play their own percussive rhythm. And you know what? It's all *acoustic* – the only acoustic music invented in the 20th century. It doesn't need amplification, the effect comes from the sheer, mesmerising volume of sound. As my temperature rises till my blood's at boiling point, I get the sense that if I stand there long enough, the centripetal force that holds my body together will give way and I will spin out of control and everything will unravel, bits of brain and bones and blood all flying off in different directions. Half delirious, my skin cells humming, I stagger back out into the open and gratefully slurp soup out of a paper cup. The Carnival blend of coconut milk and corn and split peas and spices gradually calms the vibration and returns my body temperature to normal. But I have caught the contagion and it will have to run its course.

Scene two, Mas camp. We're playing with Minshall, a designer who has single-handedly redefined the meaning of Mas, inspiring a band of acolytes who wouldn't dream of playing with anyone else. The other bands' costumes, consisting of bikinis, jockstraps and sequins, with a headdress or two thrown in, he dismisses as 'the sequin brigade'. His, by contrast, are distinctive and elaborate and instead of following a theme, they tell a story. This year, it's the legend of The Lost Tribe, in sections taken from the Qabbalah. A poster in the Mas camp explains to us that we are nomads wandering in the desert who have lost our way. We are supposed to flow across the stage on Carnival Tuesday like an endless river, or, as the poster declaims, each of us 'like a leaf blown by the winds of time'. We're in Beauty and Harmony, the section with the simplest costumes, but it takes minutes to unravel the yards and yards of white muslin, which wrap the body like a shroud with a flowing headdress. I secretly regret the bikinis and sequins, but the seriousness of the attending acolytes, the reverential atmosphere, silence me. I pay up and accept my costume.

Scene three, Panorama: the pan competition finals at the Savannah. They take a long time, because each complete orchestra has to be wheeled onto the stage and set up, play its piece, and get off again, along with a whole crowd of supporters. In the long gaps between performances, we stand around and lime, drink corn soup and beer and rum, eat shark bake and pelau, and mingle with the crowd. One minute I'm talking to a celebrated writer whose last novel I reviewed, then I'm in a group of people who are jokingly complaining about outsiders invading Carnival. A heart-stoppingly handsome man steps his whole 6 foot 4 inch self across the circle and gives me a bear hug, with the words, 'Don't mind them, we love visitors.' I have just been embraced by an invincible West Indies fast bowler I am accustomed to watching on television dispatching luckless batsmen with deadly accuracy. My delirium increases.

I'm sleep-deprived, but there's no time to sleep. We're playing J'ouvert at 2.30 am. J'ouvert is 'dirty mas' and takes place at night. It represents the devilish side of Carnival, a kind of communal exorcism, in which you daub yourself in mud or paint, and roam through the streets being devils for a night. How devilish depends on your choice of band, and the choice for us is between the one consisting of demented young men hurling black paint at you, or the one an experienced J'ouvert player advises me to opt for, having done black paint and saying never again... The mud band is the softer option. I stand in line, wearing very little, shivering in the darkness, waiting to be slapped all over with mud by a very rough man. I watch nervously as he dips his hands in a tub of gluppy stuff with which he seems to assault the woman ahead of me. I have an altogether new sensation in the gamut of sensations Carnival is throwing at me. I realise I'm scared. I've never done anything remotely like this before, and I haven't the faintest idea what to expect. Suddenly, I am next in line, slapped all over, smeared head to foot in mud, and stumbling forward to join everybody else behind the music truck. By the time a few bottles of Carib are coursing through my veins, I am ready to dance all night. We set off through the streets, dancing in a crowd, jammed up together, physical contact keeping us warm. Bodies bump and grind as we move forward, half-naked and anonymous, united by the music. After a while, I am aware that the arbitrary jostle has been replaced by a singularity of intent. Every time I move, someone behind me moves with me, not holding me exactly, but attached. I don't look back, but try a few times to shake off my escort. I step to the left, and so does he. I step to the right, he follows. His breath hot on my neck makes the hairs rise. I can no longer stop myself, and I turn my head, meeting the eyes directly in front of mine. There's no-one there. I mean, there's someone there all right, his face six inches from mine, his eyes staring, but so completely expressionless he appears possessed. He looks straight through me, as if my body too is nothing more than a vehicle, and our proximity just a physical accident. At the same time, I feel something hot and hard against my back and can't help being aware that, all along the road, dark alleys beckon... At that precise and blessed moment, I am rescued by my more experienced friend, who sizes up the situation at a glance and deftly detaches me from my incubus. The devils have been exorcised. We walk slowly home together as the sun comes up, stopping for breakfast at a roadside stall. At the house where I'm staying, someone has been posted at the back door with a saucepan to sluice us off as we come in. I stand in a stream of icy water in the early dawn, gleefully relieved I went for mud.

Carnival Monday. A day to rest before the climactic marathon of Carnival Tuesday. Just for fun, in the evening we pile into two taxis, vintage 60s British cars, with all-in-one leather seats and chrome and wood dashboards and mascots, and drive to St James. A street of rumshops hosts an ongoing street party, including pans – yes! I step out of the taxi, hear the music and turn, follow the float, and am lost... When I come to, I don't know how long afterwards, I'm wandering aimlessly in a crowd of people. Suddenly, an arm comes out of the crowd and pulls me over, and the owner says, let's dance.... I check his face for human presence, and decide to stay. Hours later, immersed in discussion in a rumshop, I realise it is nearly morning and we have to be at the Savannah at eight. I don't know where I am or how to get home, but my new friend walks me there and sees me into the sleeping house. As I close the door behind me, I catch a glimpse of him still and silent at the crossroads, early sunlight streaking the far end of the street.

Carnival Tuesday. It's the last day, when everything comes to a head in a last orgy of all-day partying, the day of 'pretty mas', the costume parades, the showing off and flaunting yourself in the street to music as you dance through Port of Spain. We struggle into our costumes, winding the yards of muslin into headpieces, wrapping ourselves in nomads' weeds, and set off for the Savannah, short of sleep, self-conscious and conspicuously white-clad in the grey of morning. As we approach the Savannah, we join rivulets of lost tribespeople wending their way to the same point, tall men with intricately woven turbans, women with fantastic designs painted on their faces and bare brown midriffs, little shells and feathers and amulets sewn into their costumes, some carrying elaborate staves hung with gourds and fetish objects. As we hunt for our section, someone mentions that there are 2,500 people in our band. Suddenly we realise what it's all about. We *are* the Lost Tribe, the people of Trinidad, with all their contradictions and violent disagreements. One man's vision comes alive in the coming together of so many of us in the costume of the band. Playing mas, I now see, is a collective statement of faith in the possibility of transcendence. At Carnival, the rivers flow into each other, just as the calypso says.

There is a long time to think about this, because nothing really happens for at least four hours, apart from standing in the sun as it gets hotter and hotter. We buy ice and wrap it in our headties to cool ourselves down. For a few moments, Minshall, a small, spry white Trinidadian of around 60, mas-man, wizard and leader of the Lost Tribe, bestows his benevolence on us. Time passes slowly, but it isn't boring because suspense is building moment by moment, and music's playing, and tassa drummers are drumming, and finally we are in Beauty and Harmony and very slowly moving towards the stage. The first sections begin to go on, preceded by the tassa drummers, then a long river of cloth carried across by a handful of dancers, then, very stately, the Patriarchs in their turbans, escorting a huge fetish totem, then we hear the announcer say, 'And this is Beauty and Harmony, the largest section', and we step onto the stage... a surge of adrenaline electrifies my body, sweeping me out there in front of all those people, and our griot is singing us across from the side of the stage and we're dancing with the cloth swirling all round us and the television cameras and the faces, and up so high we are floating over Port of Spain. And then it's over, we've crossed, the next section is filling the stage behind us, and the Lost Tribe is flowing across like leaves blown by the winds of time. I stand in the cooling spray of cold air and water and watch my band playing, and the feeling is so intense I don't know what to do with it or even how to name it, except I'm playing mas in Carnival. My feet carry me to the end of the Savannah and as I hesitate at the edge of the stream of costumed revellers, I hear drumming and a Yorùbá chorus praising Sàngó, god of lightning and electricity, and for a second, I'm totally disorientated. I have a hallucinatory moment when I'm back in a Nigerian village, attending a Sàngó festival. Then the song moves into an invocation of Sàngó's contemporary manifestations, and I find myself once again on a street in Port of Spain as a float passes with who but the Laventille Engine Room, and I step into the river and dance to the sound of a metal bar ringing on a crude metal gong. I dance all day through Port of Spain, high on adrenaline and rum, and the people on the float adopt me and give me bottles of beer. One in particular becomes my friend, and together we enter the garden of a house at the side of the road to beg for water from a very old frail lady who brings some in a bucket and we throw it over each other to cool off; my nomad's weeds are drenched and sticking to my body, but the thing is to keep going even though all I've eaten since yesterday is some honey-roasted peanuts early in the morning. Everyone talks to everyone else, and our band is like a family, and all together we arrive at Woodford Square; the whole band stops for a rest and people lie on the grass to recover before the last lap. It's getting dark. I'm part of the Laventille Engine Room entourage by now, and it turns out my protector is their singer and is known as Thunder, and last year they got to the calypso final. On we go, and I notice Thunder has an enthusiastic following of ardent young female fans, and I comment on this, and he says 'I have my followers, but I'm following you,' and by now I don't ever want the day to end and any adventure that comes my way is OK by me, so I agree to go back to Laventille with the band and I climb in the truck and off we go.

There are a lot of people in the truck, apart from the musicians. There's an elderly woman who is quite silent and still in the midst of all the noise, and Thunder tells me she's a priestess. She's there because this is an iron band, and iron belongs to Ògún. But thunder is part of the domain of Sàngó, and I think of the sparks that fly when iron is struck, and the electric surge that propelled me across the stage, and I realise there are a lot of powerful forces in this truck. I'm standing next to a young woman and when she hears I'm from Barbados she tells me she's been there, so I ask what she went there to do, and she says, 'Oh I was carrying drugs to sell.' It dawns on me that I am in a social situation for which I'm ill-equipped. I have no money left, I am wearing the remains of a carnival costume and I'm going to a part of Port of Spain which I know only by its reputation. But the adrenaline is still coursing, and when we stop somewhere still in Port of Spain, I help the band unload the truck and pack all the instruments into some battered looking vehicles, into one of which I get, along with Thunder and two or three other people, and we are heading for Laventille when suddenly Thunder stops the car and gets out, tells the driver to wait a second, and disappears. I am too high on rum and exhaustion to notice but he's away a long time, and the driver gets restless. We're parked in the middle of a street and Thunder has still not returned, when for the first time, the driver seems to notice me and asks who I am. From his expression, I can tell this is a good moment for me to get out of the car and let him go home, so I do. But what to do? I'm in the mood for an adventure, and don't feel like giving up on it so easily, so I sit on a wall and watch the trucks going by still playing music, and my friend the music expert drives by and sees me and stops. So I go with him to a bar round the corner, and he's very sympathetic, but he says it's a good thing I didn't go to Laventille, because it's a dangerous place and it's all for the best, and soon my more experienced friend from J'ouvert comes along, and she's going round the corner to her auntie's house, so I go with her. So instead of my adventure, I end up sitting safely in the auntie's living room, and then they see me back to Auntie Brenda's, and I have this absolutely enormous sense of relief at being home and I fall into bed and sleep till the next morning. And everyone tells me it was a *very* good thing I didn't go to Laventille, as anything could have happened and now I feel Thunder did me a favour by disappearing and on my way out through the airport, I buy the CD with his song on it, and listen to it when I get home, and laugh.

3:
LUIS

I met Luis in Havana. La Lisa, a working class district on the edge of the city, is a twenty-kilometre ride in a battered taxi from the centre of town, a district of shabby apartment blocks with outside staircases where life is lived on the street. I was visiting a family on the fourth floor of one these. Juan, whose family it was, led me up the stairs and along the outside landings which punctuated each stage, past the doors of other apartments. On the third floor, a door stood open, casting an oblong of light onto the concrete. It was like the mouth of a cave, and I glanced inside. A man was there, under a bright electric light, and as we passed he called out to us. 'My godfather,' said Juan, and we went inside.

I saw an elderly man in a wheelchair in a sparsely furnished room. I smiled and uttered a few of my limited store of Spanish words. He answered me in halting English, inviting me to sit down, telling me his name was Luis. As I sat, I noticed that Luis had no legs. On the wall was the faded photograph of a woman. Gesturing to it he explained, 'My mother, from Scotland.' The only other picture in the room was of Fidel. Apart from that, there was a bookcase with a few scattered books and a table with a strip light attached to it. I asked what he used it for, and he said, 'Reading and writing.' Wheeling his chair over to the bookcase, he brought me a book to demonstrate. It was a Yorùbá grammar book, printed in 1914, no doubt to assist colonial servants being posted to Nigeria. From this book, Luis was teaching himself Yorùbá.

Luis was a babalawo, a master of the word. A legless priest, confined to a priestly cell, learning a language he could share with no-one. Marooned on an island three floors up, relying on passing ships for sustenance. I asked how he lost his legs. Jumping off a building, trying to kill himself, he told me. 'Unfortunately, I survived.' His eyes were humorous and his voice warm, belying the bleakness of the words. In that case, God must have wanted you to live, I suggested. Luis flashed me a look and laughed. 'No, the doctors,' he said. 'Now I am in prison.' He wanted to kill himself when his wife left him, taking the children with her. He must have read my expression, because he deftly turned the conversation. 'Do you have a child?' Gratefully, I nodded. 'Oh then, she must be as beautiful as the mother?' It was my turn to laugh. 'Más linda,' I said, drawing the picture out of my bag. Luis looked from my daughter's face to mine and nodded. 'Más linda.' We both laughed.

Luis fought for Castro in the Congo and Angola. He had lived the revolution, and was living it still, cheerfully tragic in its contradictions. Juan, who had gone on, leaving me with Luis, now came back and asked me to go upstairs. I stayed up there for some time, eating, and looking at school books. As I came back down, I paused once again at the open door, and Luis was waiting for me. He called me to come in. He was holding something, and explained he wanted to make me a gift. On the paper he gave me was the picture of a rose, and on the back, the place and the date of our meeting, and the words: 'My modest given to you, for remember me. God blest you. Luis.' I held the paper in my hand and felt for a response. The apartment was as empty as a prison cell. My eye fell on the Yorùbá grammar, and by some trick of association I saw the grove, and the lazy brown water of the stream. 'Òsun is my goddess,' I said, 'and she would like me to give you this.' I knew as I put the note in his hand that it was nothing, but like him I had nothing else to give. But it wasn't the money that excited him. At the mention of Òsun, his eyes caught fire, and he turned his chair around and led me to a cupboard at the back of the room. Flinging open the door, he revealed two small shelves of paraphernalia, which at first I could make no sense of. It looked to my eyes like old bits of junk, dirty and worn – bits of iron, a clay pot, other objects of indeterminate status. Luis was watching me closely. 'For the worship of Òsun,' he said, and pointed, 'for Sàngó, for Elegbara.' His voice was husky, and I looked again at the ritual objects. I did not understand their purpose, while for him they were infused with meaning. But now I understood something else, which before had been lacking. Luis did not inhabit his prison cell. He was elsewhere, seated in the shrine at the centre of the grove, throwing cowries to divine the future. He had not been surprised to see me. The children of Òsun will always find each other, brought together by the currents that flow around the earth.

It was time to leave. *'Esé gaan, bàbá,'* I murmured, 'thank you.' I could tell from his response that he wasn't used to hearing Yorùbá spoken. Its meaning is in the music, which he couldn't hear. He had, after all, only the book to teach him, and silence where the music should have been. I left Luis in La Lisa, and returned to central Havana. The air was thick with an indefinable smell, a miasma born of effluent and the noxious exhaust of a million cars, choking the city. As I neared my hotel, a faint breeze blew across my face, bearing the smell of the sea.

ABOUT THE AUTHOR

Jane Bryce was born in Tanzania and studied for her doctorate in Nigeria. She joined the Cave Hill campus of the University of the West Indies in Barbados in 1992. She has a responsibility for the Department's offerings in the area of African Literature, as well as teaching courses on the novel, poetry, literature of the colonial encounter, creative writing and feminist theory/women's writing. She also teaches Caribbean literature and film. She has taught Creative Writing: Fiction since 1997, a workshop-based course designed to equip students with the skills for writing short fiction, some of which finds its way into *Poui*: the Cave Hill Journal of Creative Writing.

With other colleagues, she has been involved in initiatives to expand the opportunities for creative writing at Cave Hill. This has included summer workshops in prose fiction and poetry led by well known Caribbean writers.

Opal Palmer Adisa
Until Judgement Comes
ISBN 1 84523 042 6 £8.99

The stories in this collection move the heart and the head. They concern the mystery that is men: men of beauty who are as cane stalks swaying in the breeze, men who are afraid of and despise women, men who prey on women, men who have lost themselves, men trapped in sexual and religious guilt, men who love women and men who are searching for their humanity...

The stories are framed by the memories of an old Jamaican woman about the community that has grown up around her. The seven stories are structured around wise sayings that the community elder remembers as her grandfather's principle legacy, concerning the nature of judgement, both divine and human. Each story uses a saying as the starting point but the stories are far from illustrative tracts of that saying. From Devon aka Bad-Boy growing up with an abusive mother, to Ebenezer, a single man mysteriously giving birth to a child, to the womanizer Padee whose many women and children struggle to resolve issues with their father, each story reveals the complex, and often painful introspective search of these men.

Jennifer Rahim
Songster and Other Stories
ISBN 1 84523 048 5 £7.99

Rahim's stories move between the present and the past to make sense of the tensions between image and reality in contemporary Trinidad. The contemporary stories show the traditional, communal world in retreat before the forces of local and global capitalism. A popular local fisherman is gunned down when he challenges the closure of the beach for a private club catering to white visitors and the new elite; an internet chat room becomes a rare safe place for AIDs sufferers to make contact; cocaine has become the scourge even of the rural communities. But the stories set thirty years earlier in the narrating 'I's' childhood reveal that the 'old-time' Trinidad was already breaking up. The old pieties about nature symbolised by belief in the presence of the folk-figure of 'Papa Bois' are powerless to prevent the ruthless plunder of the forests; communal stability has already been uprooted by the pulls towards emigration, and any sense that Trinidad was ever edenic is undermined by images of the destructive power of alcohol and the casual presence of paedophilic sexual abuse.

Rahim's Trinidad, is though, as her final story makes clear, the creation of a writer who has chosen to stay, and she is highly conscious that her perspective is very different from those who have taken home away in a suitcase, or who visit once a year. Her Trinidad is 'not a world in my head like a fantasy', but the island that 'lives and moves in the bloodstream'. Her reflection on the nature of small island life is as fierce and perceptive as Jamaica Kincaid's *A Small Place,* but comes from and arrives at a quite opposite place. What Rahim finds in her island is a certain existential insouciance and the capacity of its people, whatever their material circumstance, to commit to life in the knowledge of its bitter-sweetness.

OTHER SHORT STORY COLLECTIONS YOU MIGHT LIKE

Hazel Campbell, *Singerman,* **0-948833-44-0, £6.99**
Realistic and magical, sombre and comic, heroic and ironic, these stories explore Jamaican reality through a variety of voices and forms, connecting the slave past and contemporary gang warfare.

Kwame Dawes, *A Place to Hide,* **1-900715-48-1, £9.99**
Dawes's characters are driven by their need for intimate contact: with people, with God, with their creative potential. Their stories give an incisive portrayal of contemporary Jamaica that is unsparing in confronting its elements of misogyny & violence.

Meiling Jin, *Song of the Boatwoman,* **0-948833-86-6, £6.95**
These stories, set in Guyana, London, America, Malaysia and China, explore the inner lives of women of the Chinese diaspora, lesbian sexuality and racism.

Rabindranath Maharaj, *The Writer and his Wife,* **0-948833-81-5, £7.99**
Maharaj's Trinidadian characters struggle heroically, though sometimes comically, to make their mark on the earth. It is as if the more frustrating their outward circumstances, the more intense their inner lives.

E.A. Markham, *Taking the Drawing Room Through Customs,* **1-900715-69-4, £9.99**
Whether writing with observant humour, occasional bleakness, audacious mythologising or absurdist magical realism, the crafted completeness of the stories in this collection reveal Markham as a master of the short story form.

Alecia McKenzie, *Stories from Yard,* **1-900715-62-7, £7.99**
Fear and bitterness pollute the ground from which the young female characters of these stories must struggle to grow. With many 'bad seeds' of sexual violence, lies and prejudice taking root around them, their blossoming, though determined, is always under threat.

Geoffrey Philp, *Uncle Obadiah and the Alien,* **1-900715-01-5, £6.99**
Drawing on rasta and ragamuffin flavours, science fiction and tall tales, these short stories set in Jamaica and Miami have humour and pathos in their explorations of families, race, class and sexual orientation.

N.D. Williams, *Julie Mango,* **1-900715-77-5, £9.99**
Williams's characters want the space to cultivate their sense of individual worth, though this can sometimes involve becoming trapped in an absurd or confining persona. At the heart of all the stories is the plea for a humane tolerance.

All Peepal Tree titles are available from our website:
www.peepaltreepress.com

Explore our list of over 170 titles, read sample poems and reviews, discover new authors, established names and access a wealth of information about books, authors and Caribbean writing. Secure credit card ordering, fast delivery throughout the world at cost or less.

You can contact us at:
Peepal Tree Press, 17 King's Avenue, Leeds LS6 1QS, United Kingdom
Tel: +44 (0) 113 2451703 E-mail: hannah@peepaltreepress.com